GALLOPING HEARTS

Sasha's life is spent at her aunt's stables. But when they are taken over by handsome Seth Marston and her horse sold to dissolute showjumper Guy Palmer, her world is turned upside down. Sasha is overwhelmed by her feelings for Seth and leaves to work for Guy. Her confusion intensifies as Seth pursues her, fairytale-style. But when Guy mistreats Sasha's horse, and Seth comes to the rescue, will Sasha finally stop running and embrace a happy ending with Seth?

JUDE WINTER

GALLOPING HEARTS

Complete and Unabridged

LINFORD
Leicester

First published in Great Britain in 2011

First Linford Edition
published 2012

British Library CIP Data

Winter, Jude.
    Galloping hearts. - - (Linford romance library)
    1. Love stories.
    2. Large type books.
    I. Title II. Series
    823.9'2–dc23

    ISBN 978–1–4448–1255–8

Published by
F. A. Thorpe (Publishing)
Anstey, Leicestershire

Set by Words & Graphics Ltd.
Anstey, Leicestershire
Printed and bound in Great Britain by
T. J. International Ltd., Padstow, Cornwall

This book is printed on acid-free paper

1

Sasha flung the ancient car round the bends of the narrow lane. Although it was her day off, she was keen to get to the stable and surprise Aunt Libby with the present she had spent most of the morning choosing. Her aunt was not one to make much of her birthday — left to herself, she would carry on just as on any other day — which was why it was so important to Sasha to make the occasion special in some way: a small thank you for all the older woman had done for her over the years.

The window was jammed open on the old Volvo estate; had been through all the freezing winter weather. It was just one of the many sacrifices she and her aunt had made in order to keep Old Oak Stables running now business was dwindling away. As she reached the ancient hollow oak tree that gave the stables its name, and steered round the pot holes in the yard, Sasha felt the sun on her hand for the first time this year. Welcome as it was, the golden light seemed to highlight the shabbiness of the stables: corrugated iron used to patch up gaps in the tiles, weeds sprouting up through the paving slabs, rusty troughs, sagging doors. No wonder they weren't getting the new business they desperately needed.

Sasha had taken one hand from the steering wheel and was pushing her sleek, dark hair out of her eyes when a huge, top-of-the-range horse box came roaring out of the back yard. She swerved from its path, stopped the car and turned her head to stare after it; wondering what it was doing here. As far as she knew, they were expecting no new arrivals: they could hardly afford to feed the animals they already had.

She sighed and then, pushing her worries to the back of her mind, started to prepare for Aunty Libby's birthday surprise.

The cake was in the shape of a horse's head with long curly chocolate mane, and glossy caramel coat. Sasha's closest friend, Anna, was starting up her own baking business and had been up into the small hours decorating it for her aunt. Sasha put the cake on the long bonnet of the car, shielding it with her waterproof jacket as she lit six candles: one for each decade. Aunty Libby, sixty years old today! No wonder she was finding it harder to manage the work here. Although her aunt would be the last person to admit that she was struggling, it was obvious to Sasha. When they were mucking out the stables, her aunt couldn't manage a half-full wheelbarrow any more. She even stumbled under the weight of a large saddle.

As she sheltered the flickering candles, Sasha's mind once again turned over her worries. How long could they could keep going? What would happen to the horses? What would happen to her and her aunt?

Not now, she cautioned herself, *this*

is a happy day. Sasha forced a wide smile onto her face, which took root the moment she focussed on the nature of the occasion. And then, present tucked under one arm, cake held out in front of her, she moved across the yard toward the open loose box where she knew she would find her aunt working.

'Happy birthday to you, happy birthday to you!' she sang in a discordant but cheerful voice as she peered into the gloomy stable. 'Happy birthday, dear Aunt Libby, happy birthday to you.'

The hunched figure pressed into the farthest corner of the loose box looked far from celebratory. Always small, the combination of the forlorn stance and the clustering shadows made her aunt appear dramatically frail and elderly as well. Sasha checked the candles, gulped down her worries and advanced into the stable, hands outstretched. The candles were still alight but made little impression on the gloom of the building.

Her aunt snatched a glance at the

4

cake and then looked away. Sasha could see a tear glistening in the candlelight.

She knew that her fiercely private aunt would feel uncomfortable at being disturbed in an emotional moment, and so she decided to make light of the situation.

'Libby, what's wrong? Did you think I'd forgotten your birthday? Were you hoping for a surprise party this year with us all jumping out of the hay barn and shouting 'Surprise' at the tops of our voices?' she joked, knowing that any large scale celebration would be the last thing her aunt would want. 'Well, I'll do my best next year.'

'Over my dead body, you will,' growled Libby.

'Come on, blow out your candles. You only have to put up with this one day a year, so the least you can do is to be polite and make the effort.' She stood right in front of Libby, cake held at perfect candle-blowing height. 'If you don't get a move on, I'll be forced to start singing again,' she teased in a sing-song voice.

'Anything to get you off my back.' Aunt Libby blew a huge breath which finished off the candles and roused all the surrounding dust.

When Sasha had finished spluttering, she balanced the cake on one arm and took her aunt's hand.

'Come on, have a break and get the kettle on and then I'll cut the cake for us. Should be a good one. It's got that white chocolate filling you love,' she wheedled, as though tempting a child.

'Sasha — I'm not really in the mood for it, I'm sorry. I can see you've gone to a lot of trouble as usual and the cake's a work of art, but I'm not feeling too upbeat.'

The older woman trailed off, retrieved her spade and fork and turned her back on her niece to continue sifting through the straw.

Her aunt was right; the cake was a work of art, and Sasha was not prepared to give up. What sort of a niece would leave her aunt close to tears and slaving on her sixtieth birthday? She squared her jaw and moved closer; this time to touch her aunt's shoulder, bony and birdlike.

'It's okay. Just humour me for ten minutes. Open the present and the card, pretend to eat a slice of cake; you don't even need to smile if you can't manage it. And then I'll get going and leave you alone to be as miserable as you want, I promise.'

★ ★ ★

Once in the low kitchen of the ramshackle grooms' cottage they shared, Sasha found a knife and started to cut through the poor unwanted cake. She cut two slices and then looked up. 'By the way, who was driving that horse box? Not exactly the safest driver.'

There was a bang and a splash as her aunt dropped the full kettle onto the tiled floor. Sasha jumped up to find a mop, while her aunt stood staring down at the widening pool of water, as though frozen to the spot.

'Libby, there's something really wrong, isn't there? Is there anything I can do to help? I know you like to keep things to yourself, but a problem shared and all that . . . '

Sasha finished mopping up the water, refilled the kettle and then took her aunt's hand and pulled her down into a wooden chair. 'Talk to me, please,' she ordered.

'You're the last person I'd want to talk to about what I've just had to do.' Libby rubbed her weatherbeaten forehead with her hand. 'I didn't think you'd be in today. Forgotten it was my birthday and you'd have to make a fuss of me.' She looked across at the younger girl, and shook her head fondly.

'Libby, you're beginning to scare me. Can you just tell me what's happened?' Sasha sat down at the table opposite her aunt and cupped her pointed face in her hands, long fingers pressing into her prominent cheekbones, eyes full of worry.

'Sweetheart, it's about money, that's all — or the lack of it.' Her aunt narrowed her grey eyes. 'It's getting to breaking point for the stables and you know it — we both do. No customers, too many old horses that don't earn their keep but still need to eat. I'm not a worrier by nature but it's getting to the stage where I can't sleep at nights for thinking about what's going to happen to all the horses if things don't start to improve.'

Her aunt's words tailed off into a whisper. 'So I did what I had to do to buy us some time. I'm sorry, sweetheart, but I was offered a great deal for Jasmine and for all our sakes, I accepted it. That was her leaving in the horse box that passed you by.'

Hearing the news, Sasha was consumed with a childlike rage. She wanted to stamp her foot and scream, 'it's not fair' at her aunt, in a way she never had; not even in childhood.

She closed her dark eyes, took a deep breath and said in a flat voice, 'But I thought she was mine.'

Jasmine, or Winter Jasmine as she was registered, was a five-year-old Arabian mare. She had been acquired as a frightened foal by the stables, after an animal charity had prosecuted her former owner for extreme cruelty. The gawky foal had been terrified of human contact but after a few months of gentle handling from Sasha and her aunt, the filly had learned to trust again.

Libby had entrusted the highly-bred horse to Sasha, letting her break in the young animal herself. Only a few months ago, Sasha had started to ride Jasmine and had anticipated a wonderful life-long partnership with the beautiful Arab mare.

'I know that, Sasha. Why do you think I dreaded telling you? Why do you think I was blubbing in the stables when you surprised me just now? Takes a lot to make me cry, doesn't it?' Libby brushed her short grey hair off her forehead. 'It was just the size of the offer, sweetheart, it was too much to refuse. It's enough to keep the stables going for a couple of months and I'm going to go all out on the marketing — get in touch with the local papers, organise a few events, get the white-wash out and smarten the place up. Don't you see? Selling Jasmine has given us one last chance to turn things round.'

Sasha couldn't meet her aunt's eyes. 'Why did you do it all behind my back? Why didn't you tell me? At least I could have said goodbye to her. And maybe I could have found some way to raise the money for her myself.' Her dark eyes were glistening with unshed tears.

'I thought and thought about it and decided that this would be the kindest way. You could never have raised the money, any more than I could, and as for saying goodbye — you would never have been able to let go of her. No, this was the best way.'

Sasha pushed away the plate of cake and fiddled with her hair, desperate to regain control of her runaway emotions.

She remembered the last time she had seen the mare. Jasmine had been nuzzling her shoulder over the gate by the hay barn, total trust apparent in her huge mild eyes.

'Libby, I'm trying to be mature and reasonable about this but I'm not doing too well. It feels as if you've got rid of my best friend. I taught her to trust me — and then I wasn't there for her. At least tell me where she's gone. I need convincing that she'll be happy.'

'Of course she's gone to a good home. I would never have agreed to sell her, otherwise — you know what I'm like. It's rather a prestigious home, actually — Guy Palmer, the celebrity showjumper. He saw her at the Welsley show — do you remember, where you won that Inhand class? And he's got this idea into his head that he's going to take a pure-bred Arab to the top. Don't understand why, but it's always been a dream of his, apparently.' Aunt Libby looked baffled at the whim she described.

'I don't know if she'd enjoy that. She's not a natural jumper, I don't think. He could have got a horse with much more raw talent — I wouldn't have thought she's got the temperament for it.' Sasha sounded like an anxious parent. 'You did tell him about her background? That she'd been abused, and rescued as a yearling?'

'Of course I did, Sash. Actually that was one of the reasons he was so desperate for her and why I agreed to sell her.'

Sasha creased her forehead, 'I don't get it.'

'Well, I didn't at first, but he explained to me that if he took a horse with Jasmine's sad history to the top, then it would be an even greater achievement. And then — and this was the bit that appealed to me — he said he'd give his first year's winnings to a horse charity of my choice.'

Sasha, subdued by this evidence of worthiness, nodded in silence, her tears still flowing as she digested the news.

'Sasha, he is such a nice man, can't you see that Jasmine couldn't be going to a better home? He will really use her potential, and she could end up a celebrity herself. Not bad for the skinny little foal who spooked at her own shadow, is it?'

Libby's expression remained no-nonsense, but the pleading of her voice suggested that she needed her niece to understand.

Sasha's couldn't help feeling sympathy for her aunt but she kept her eyes downwards as her tears splashed onto the table. After a long moment, she reached into her pocket, found a screwed-up tissue and rubbed angrily at her eyes.

'I need to give you this.' She stood up and tossed the present, elaborately wrapped in gold paper and pink ribbons, to her aunt. 'I have to be on my own now.'

As she opened the latch of the small wooden door, a dark grey car was arriving in the yard. Sasha's only driving experience was the battered Volvo, and she had never been the least interested in cars, but the unusual streamlined shape of this one caught her eye. She had no idea of the make or model, but it was evidently expensive and suggested sophistication; the kind of car driven more usually by James Bond than by customers of Old Oak Riding School.

As the car parked beside her own, her instinct was to head off into the barn behind the stables and leave her aunt to deal with whoever it was; she simply felt she couldn't face polite small talk just now. But when the car door swung open and some elegantly stitched leather shoes were followed out the car by well-cut jeans filled by well muscled long legs, her curiosity caused her to hesitate.

She pulled her hair away from her face into a temporary knot at the back of head, and she wiped her eyes with the back of her hand. Beauty preparations performed, she stood, hands on the hips of her faded jeans, watching the broad dark figure stride towards her, the glimmer of a smile on his tawny face.

'Hi there — I wonder if you can help? I'm looking for the owner of these stables.' His tone was steady and his grey eyes flicked up and down to assess her as he spoke.

'Can I ask what it's in connection with?' asked Sasha in formal tones. She wanted to be prepared, in case this was another shock sprung on her by her aunt today.

'Certainly; it's a business matter.' He glanced over her shoulder at the cottage door, as if willing her out of his way, and Sasha wondered if this was something to do with Guy Palmer. Perhaps this man was bringing over a large cheque or picking up a receipt. She couldn't think of any other business that would attract such a high-class visitor.

'Could you be a little more specific?' she said in icy tones.

He took a step backwards and raised his arched eyebrows in mock surprise. 'No, I'm afraid I couldn't at this time.

16

You see, the matter in question is confidential.'

She was irritated by his smooth manner. 'Your business wouldn't concern a certain well-bred Arabian filly, acquired from these stables, for a large sum of money, earlier today?'

He put his head on one side, regarding her with puzzled eyes and a slow smile. 'No, it has absolutely nothing to do with a certain well-bred filly — although I wish it did, by the sound of her.'

'Then why are you here?' Sasha found herself perversely enjoying this pointless deadlock; it was somewhere she could dump her frustration over the sudden loss of her horse.

'I told you it's confidential. I don't know who you are, or who you think I am, but I need to speak to the owner of the stables, whoever he or she is — to be perfectly honest, I don't have a clue — and,' his mouth twitched upwards at the edges, 'I come in peace.'

'It's all very well to say you come in

peace but unless you can be a bit more specific about the nature of your business, I am going to have to ask you to come back some other time. It's not convenient for my aunt to see you now.' She dug her hands into her pockets and squared her elfin jaw. He could do all the eyebrow-raising and lip-twitching he wanted; she wasn't going to budge.

'Are you always this hard-nosed or have I offended you in some way?' His head was now tilted at an angle, expressing confusion, and Sasha was drawn to the sculptural quality of his profile with that high-bridged nose and the broad cheekbones. The fight seemed to leave her body and she gazed in silence.

'Hello?' His voice was rich with humour.

'Sorry, I was miles away. Don't mind me. Having a bad day,' she muttered. 'I'll just get my aunt.' She banged on the cottage door and before it had opened, made a dash for her car without looking back.

2

'So who was he?' asked Sasha at the first opportunity. 'The man from yesterday.'

'The Man from Yesterday,' chuckled Libby as she opened up the tack room. 'That makes him sound quite mysterious, like *The Man from UNCLE*.' She jiggled the huge rusty key until it fitted into the lock.

'And is he?' Sasha stamped her feet to warm them as she waited for the door to open. Although officially spring, there had been a heavy frost that morning.

'Is he what?' Libby scraped the door open and turned on the light, illuminating a heavy shroud of cobwebs hanging from the rafters. 'Right, who do we need? Let's think.'

'Aunt Libby, are you doing this on purpose?' Sasha grabbed her aunt's arm in frustration.

'What? I'm just trying to remember who we need today — I'm not feeling very organised, I'm afraid.' Libby put her hand on her forehead and frowned.

Immediately, Sasha put her curiosity to one side. 'Are you all right, Aunty? You're not still worrying about Jasmine, are you? I know it was tough, I know you wouldn't have done it unless it was necessary. And what I am going to do is find a way to buy her back from the celebrity showjumper one day — but in the meantime it's okay, really it is.'

Libby let go of the bridle she was reaching for, and turned to her niece, a fond smile enveloping her creased face. 'This is the closest I am going to get to soppy, but you really are a sweetie. Just like your mother all over again. I don't know what I did to deserve you.'

'Whatever you did, you're not getting rid of me now. And I'm not fishing for compliments or anything, but after I left so dramatically yesterday, did you find time to open the present I gave you?'

Libby rolled her eyes, 'Oh, Sasha, I completely forgot. I am so sorry, and that lovely cake's still sitting there. I had my mind on other things after you left, I'm afraid. The moment we've finished here, come across and open it with me and maybe even light the candles again and I promise I will be a better birthday girl, or rather very old lady, today.'

'Nothing I'd like better. But you still haven't answered my question. The man from yesterday. Who was he? Very flash car, well spoken, expensive . . . ' Sasha trailed off as her aunt's smile grew wider.

'And handsome,' Libby finished.

'I didn't notice.' And, in answer to her aunt's look of disbelief, 'No, honestly, I was too caught up in giving him the third degree about Jasmine.' And when her aunt put her head on one side and continued to smile, 'Oh, all right, he was very good-looking. Just not my type.'

Libby snorted. 'Oh really? And when

did you discover your type?'

Sasha looked thoughtful for a moment, then turned on her aunt in exasperation. 'Let's save that conversation for another day. You're doing it again, trying to change the subject.' She spoke clearly, with great pauses between each word. 'Who . . . was . . . the . . . man . . . from . . . yesterday, and what was his business here?'

'You don't let up, do you? I think your grandad must have been a terrier. And I've no idea what you are going to say when I tell you.' Her aunt spoke to the floor.

'Spit it out. Can't be worse than yesterday's bombshell.' Sasha's mind was already racing but her expression remained composed.

'He wanted to buy the yard.' Libby's voice was flat and she kicked her heels into the concrete.

'What? You're joking!' Sasha stepped out of the door, and moved her eyes quickly around the yard, observing the buildings, the horses, and recalling the memories. Letting her eyes linger on the ancient hollow oak tree she had played in as a child. This was the only home she could remember, and she had to take several deep breaths to quell her mounting panic.

'I hope you told him where he could put his offer,' she said finally in a small voice.

Libby put a hand on her shoulder. 'I didn't, love. We haven't started talking figures yet, or any sort of timescale, but in principle I agreed. I don't have any choice, Sasha. I can't afford to keep this place going and, even if I could, I can't keep working any longer. I'm too old for this line of work and we both know it.'

'But I'm not. You could step back, Libby, take more days off, get involved in the organisation and marketing — goodness knows, one of us needs to — and leave me to do the donkey work. I was going to suggest that anyway — in fact I was thinking about it when I put the candles on your birthday cake yesterday.' Her voice was bright, but her eyes were beseechingly intense.

'Too late, I've agreed to sell. Sasha, this isn't much of a life for a pretty young girl like you. You don't have enough money to go out, or buy fashionable clothes or have holidays. I'm not surprised that you don't know what kind of man your type is, because you never have time to meet any — you're too busy slaving around here for me. I've felt bad about it for a long time.'

'But I love it here, I've always worked here, it's my life, I — '

'Well, it's time you tried something new. Even if it is with horses, work for someone who can pay you a bit more and for shorter hours. No, Sasha, my mind is made up. Seth Marston didn't need to talk me into anything; I was agreeing before he'd even finished his first sentence. I snapped his hand off, in fact!' Libby put a bridle over her arm and then reached for the saddle. 'Come on, we've got work to do. I'm taking the nine o'clock lesson in the school today, and I told Seth that you would take him out for a ride and show him around.'

'You did what? I don't want to ride with some stuck-up man who thinks he can get anything he wants just by waving a fat wad of money. He just thinks if he turns up in that expensive car, everyone will swoon and fall at his feet, well, he can think again. I bet he — '

'Sasha . . . ' Libby muttered, her alarmed eyes travelling over her niece's shoulder and out into the yard.

'And what do you know about him, anyway? Oh sure, he makes a good first impression — mainly due to a suave manner that his parents bought for him at public school, no doubt. Then there's his expensively maintained good looks. I bet he's the sort of man who spends half his life at the gym with his exclusive personal trainer and the other half with his personal shopper gathering clothes for that casual but groomed look. What's more — ' Sasha was beginning to enjoy herself — 'this stable is probably just a little toy for him, a pastime, something to keep him amused because he doesn't have to occupy himself making money and he's getting a little bit bored with City life and thinks it might make a change to discover his real man roots in the countryside.'

'And would you recommend it?' A man's voice rose from close behind her, soft with amusement.

She whirled round to see the Man from Yesterday standing smiling in the yard. Unwilling to let him witness her discomfort, she gave only a brief nod of acknowledgement and continued spiritedly, 'Yes, I would recommend it, but, you see, it's the only life I've ever known. I've always lived with my aunt at Old Oak and, since I was a small child, I've not only ridden the ponies, but looked after them and loved them. So I'm sorry that you overheard my outburst — as my aunt will tell you, I'm good at ranting — but it's an understandable reaction to the shocking news I've just been given: that the

26

place I have always considered my home, is no longer mine.'

As Sasha spoke, she tried to contain the emotion that was threatening to overwhelm her: her voice was unnaturally level and her lip trembled as she spoke. She saw the man's smile disappear, to be replaced by a look of sympathy as she articulated her distress. When she had finished, there was a short pause during which he gazed at her thoughtfully.

In the silence, Sasha tried to maintain eye contact but found that under the intensity of his regard, she was eventually forced to drop her eyes to the ground. She felt a heat circulating through her body which was several degrees higher than a mere glow of embarrassment.

'We haven't been formally introduced, but I'm Seth and I believe you are Sasha. I think I might be right in thinking that your aunt has not had time to fill you in on the details of the offer I put to her.' He looked inquiringly towards Libby, who was leaning in a dusty alcove, a saddle and bridle on her arm.

'That's right. I'd just told her the news and she went off on one, the way I told you she would, and then you arrived.' Her aunt was chuckling in a way that felt faintly disloyal to Sasha. Was she already a shared joke between this smooth interloper and her aunt?

He looked back at Sasha, his eyes crinkling up at the corners as he asked, 'And did they do a good job, do you think?'

Sasha cast her mind back but could make no sense of the question. 'I'm sorry?' she inquired.

His eyes twinkled. 'The public school, the personal trainer and that shopper of mine. Are they worth the large sums of money I pay them?'

She returned his gaze, determined not to back down this time. 'Well, depends how much they get, doesn't it? And what they had to work with in the first place. Was the raw material any good? What is it you say, Aunt Libby? You can't make a silk purse out of a sow's ear.'

The man gave a sudden deep laugh and shook his head at her. 'If you could just grit your teeth and put up with my brash company for a while longer, I would be able to run through the offer I put to your aunt yesterday. It does concern you as well.'

He brushed his hand lightly over her arm and, although not usually the nervous type, she started. His touch generated that same sensation of heat. She found herself nodding, momentarily lost for words.

'Perhaps you know that I bought the Manor House on the hill about six months ago. Since then, I've been stuck inside trying to make it habitable again, and now finally I feel like I'm winning.'

Sasha snatched a glance at Seth: he didn't look like a man who would get his hands dirty. She eyed his large hands with the long, angular fingers and the clean nails, imagined them at work, and once again felt unaccountably flustered.

'You did the work yourself?' she said after a pause.

'No one was more surprised than me, but yes, I did the work myself. I had very good advice, and I enjoyed it — I was in the mood to get stuck into something physical. Now I've reached the point where I have had to hand over to the experts and I'm at a bit of a loose end.'

'Ah, I see.' Sasha gave a sweet smile, 'You were at a loose end and decided to buy yourself a new project.' She mimicked an unconvincing posh voice. 'Oh, my dear, haven't I told you? I've taken on a quaint little riding school down the road from my house. It passes the time, you know, a little hobby for me.'

'Sasha,' hissed her aunt.

'If I had the time I'd give you a more comprehensive explanation but, right now, yours will have to do because there is more than a grain of truth in your ridicule.' He gave her a level glance and stood in front of her with his hands by his sides, as if open to any criticism she cared to throw at him. 'It was rather like that. I knew that your stables and pastures had once belonged to the Manor House, that's common knowledge. My property stops rather abruptly — '

'How unfortunate for you,' interrupted Sasha now with more humour than scorn.

'Well, yes, it was a little.' He didn't flinch. 'And so I started to research your stables and learned that they were generally run down and could do with a huge cash injection to generate more business. And then I asked around locally and the consensus was that the owner was longing to retire but had no plan in place for her animals, or for herself and her niece for that matter, and that she might be quite approachable if I could come up with a good offer.'

Sasha considered taking offence at

his description of the stables but, looking round, decided that it was simply accurate. 'So you come down here and immediately bump into some mad woman muttering on about an Arabian filly, quizzing you about your intentions and barring all access to the owner?' she teased and, when he smiled in response, noticed with pleasure that his eyes again crinkled up at the outer corners.

'I did spend a brief half hour researching the price of property and land and the growth potential for a well-equipped riding school, and then, yes, I came down here, and when I was eventually passed through the first degree, the owner greeted me in a friendly fashion and accepted my offer like a dream come true.'

'That's right, Sasha,' her aunt put in. 'I've been worried sick about what to do with this place. What with property slumping, I'm never going to get a good price for the stables in this state. And if I did sell, then you're left high and dry, not to mention the horses — too many rescues that I haven't had the time to bring on, old crocks . . . you know.'

'And why is he any different?' Sasha muttered to her aunt, her shoulder turned to exclude Seth from the conversation. 'He doesn't look the sort of man who'd be happy to feed and keep all our charity cases in his new revamped business. Can't you see, the moment the deal is done, he'll be straight on the phone to the meat man?'

'Give me a bit of credit, Sasha.' Her aunt clenched her jaw and when Sasha saw a vein pulsing in her neck, she wondered guiltily whether she'd gone too far. 'I know I'm getting on, but I haven't lost my marbles quite yet. Seth has agreed to keep on all my horses. Nothing will be sold without your say-so.'

'My say-so?'

'You're part of the deal. He's keeping you on to manage this place. You can live in our cottage, get a proper wage, and with the money from the sale, I can find somewhere nearby and slow down a little.'

'And what if I don't want to work for anyone else? What if I don't want to be sold along with the horses and buildings?' snapped Sasha, regarding the idea of her aunt's retirement as tantamount to desertion.

'Then you are perfectly entitled to leave and do whatever you want,' growled Seth, who also seemed to have lost patience with her. 'Can't you see? I have no interest in keeping you on. I can run an ad in the paper and choose from a vast number of fully experienced candidates. You are nothing to me.' His words made Sasha squirm. 'Your aunt made your continued employment a con-dition of the deal because she cares about you — but don't flatter yourself, you're hardly indispensible to me. If you don't like the terms of your employ-ment, then leave the moment contracts are exchanged.'

'For goodness' sake, Sasha, get a grip. Can't you see that Seth is doing us a huge favour? This whole deal is set out on my terms; *our* terms.' Aunt Libby was close to raging.

Sasha gulped.

'I'm sorry. I must have got so carried away with the idea of being a vulnerable heroine sold as a chattel, that I completely missed the point. I see, now it's been pointed out to me with a sledgehammer, that you are treating us very generously and I hope I can be a bit more grateful.'

She looked down at her boots and reluctantly relinquished the colourful image of herself, in a long floaty dress, being sold against her will to haughty Lord Seth.

'Gratitude? Surely not. Don't get carried away.' Seth watched her, a quizzical expression on his face, and Sasha was aware of laughter deep in his body, causing his muscular chest to swell and his broad shoulders to sway. She felt breathless and had to look away until she had regained her composure. *Focus*, she told herself sternly and forced herself to address this over-poweringly masculine presence merely as a potential employer who warranted her courtesy.

'I really am sorry I've been rude. It's just come as a bit of a shock. I know it's very short-sighted of me but I honestly hadn't imagined things ever changing here — probably because it really is the only life I've ever known. I do assure you, you will have my complete co-operation from now on — and,' she gave a nervous smile and twiddled with a stray strand of hair, 'If I haven't already burned my bridges I would love to work with you to get Old Oak Stables back on its feet.'

Seth let a gentle smile light his face and then nodded slowly. 'I admire your honesty and I can absolutely assure you that all our bridges are more than intact. Now, if you can just hang onto that attitude for another hour or two, and take me on that ride your aunt sug-gested, I would be absolutely delighted.'

He waited expectantly and Sasha

again had to grope for a reply. She couldn't disagree because she had already promised co-operation, but she was unwilling to spend time alone with a man who reduced her to a tongue-tied state she had hoped she had left behind in adolescence.

She was aware of the pressure of the silence: Libby cleared her throat anxiously several times and Seth began a comedy hum. When Sasha finally forced out an answer, a one-syllable squeak of 'Yes', she could feel her companions' relief.

'Would you like a hand getting the horses ready?' inquired Seth. 'Perhaps you could use the time to give me a few useful pointers to pass on to my personal shopper and trainer.'

3

Ambling down the high-hedged lane, a spring breeze cooling her face and the gentle clopping of the horses' hooves in her ears, Sasha felt as if she could breathe again: the mild outdoors was a world away from the tension of the tack room. Even though Seth had assured her that he was an experienced rider, they were both riding reliable horses. Sasha was leading the way, letting her reins relax in the quiet lane, assured by the sound of hooves that Seth was following close behind. While the lane was narrow, there was no chance of riding two abreast and Sasha sagged in relief in the absence of the magnetic eye contact she had just endured in the stable yard.

Although she would not have admitted it to Seth, for the first time that spring — safe in the new knowledge

38

that the future of the yard, her aunt and the horses was assured — she was able to relax and enjoy the feel of the countryside. And the prospect of a challenging position of responsibility in a stable with resources also contributed to her improved mood. As she gazed ahead between Oscar's pricked grey ears, she was already imagining the improvements she could make with even a small addition to the budget.

She was keen to prolong this companionable silence for as long as possible but after a few minutes Seth began to speak. He wasn't shouting, but he must have possessed an actor's power of projection because his voice carried easily despite the distance between them.

'Have you always worked here with your aunt?' he asked.

'I've lived here for about as long as I can remember. My parents died in a car accident when I was five, so Aunty Libby, my mother's older sister, took me in.' She didn't shout either because she had no wish for her revelations on such a sensitive subject to be heard, but the breeze must have been travelling in Seth's direction and her words, too, carried.

'Oh — I'm sorry.'

'Don't be. It was a long time ago.' Yet all these years later, the death of her parents was still not something that she could transform into small talk; she could never numb the ache that lay behind her calm words.

'No, I meant that I'm sorry for asking. I assumed it was a casual, work-related question and I certainly didn't mean to pry.' Seth's words carried none of the pity she had learned to dread.

They continued in silence, the clinking of the bit and the rhythm of the hooves lulling Sasha as Seth's matter-of-fact tone continued to echo in her ears, hinting at an unusually understanding audience for her most innermost thoughts.

She cleared her throat. 'Aunt Libby has been wonderful and we're every-thing to each other, but even so I sometimes allow myself to wonder what it would have been like if . . . you know . . . if my parents were still alive. And the moment I let in a chink of self-pity, I'm lost. Sad and sorry for myself, sobbing at what might have been and how different I could have been if I'd been brought up by my mother and father. And it's nonsense, really — Aunt Libby couldn't have been kinder. She was childless by choice, just devoted to horses, not that bothered about humans, but she turned her life around entirely for me to try to compensate for my loss. It's just that it's not quite the same if it's your aunt, is it?'

'No, no, it isn't. I can see that, and I think you're being a bit hard on yourself describing your longing as self pity. But if that attitude keeps you strong and happy — '

'Exactly,' she interrupted. 'So no sympathy, please. I don't like it. Now, my turn. What made you come down here? You don't look like the type to want to downsize and keep chickens, or the hunting, shooting, fishing kind either, so what was it?'

'A motorway accident.'

A pheasant leapt into their path, causing both horses to spook. Sasha quickly regained control of Oscar and turned to see her companion's horse backing into the hedgerow. Before Seth could master his expression, she caught a glimpse of raw panic in his eyes.

Calmly, she walked Oscar level with the frightened horse and grabbed the reins until he was steady. After soothing the horse, her eyes moved upwards to Seth, his face by now a neutral mask.

'How did a car accident make you want to be a riding stable owner?'

Seth gave a grin which she could detect out of the corner of her eye. 'Sounds strange, doesn't it? But I had a complete life carved out for myself in the City, an internet business that was doing pretty well, had been for some years. A nice flat in a central location, a long-term girlfriend whom I assumed I would one day marry.'

They had begun to move forward again and the path had widened, allowing them to ride abreast. At the mention of a girlfriend, Sasha met Seth's eyes and nodded warmly. For some reason it felt important to demonstrate how little the existence of another woman bothered her. 'Sounds good,' she said, to convey her tolerance.

'I hadn't given it a lot of thought, honestly. I didn't reflect on anything, I was too busy to analyse but, looking back, I suppose I was vaguely dissatisfied — just not enough so to do anything about it.

'And then one day, travelling between Manchester and London in heavy rain, there was a pile-up in the central lane. A lorry skidded sideways and blocked all three lanes and, you know how it is, everyone was ignoring the speed restrictions and was going too fast. The cars crashed into the lorry and the vehicles behind crashed into the cars and so it went on. To anyone watching it must have looked like total mayhem. But I wasn't watching — I was the second car in the pile-up, I was driving much too fast, on automatic pilot, and I went straight into the lorry.'

'Oh, no. What happened?' Sasha was struck by Seth's straight narration of the horrific events. He didn't play it for drama, he was just keen to communicate something significant.

'Well, I'm still here. And that was a miracle, according to the emergency crew working flat out to get us out of the wreckage. My car had spun out, turned every sort of somersault going and ended up stuck in the central reservation. And yet I didn't have a scratch — well, I needed a couple of stitches in my hand, and that was all. My car, on the other hand, was a crumpled wreck. And that, bizarrely, is how I came to be here disrupting your life. I had one of those road-to-Damascus moments. It struck me just how quickly it all could be snatched away, and how precious life is.'

'And that you could be living it

differently?' Sasha asked, forgetting the effect on her life, just fascinated with the story itself.

'Yeah.' He made a mock grimace. 'My girlfriend had teased me for years, believed in treating me mean and keeping me keen I guess, and I suddenly realised that I *wasn't* all that keen. I definitely wasn't in love with her. It was just a habit, a way of passing the time. And yet this was the woman I had assumed I would be marrying — that's how little I had considered my life. And my business — it bored me. I'd loved the challenge of setting it up, but I wasn't remotely interested in pushing it any further, and maintaining the status quo just involved going through the motions. Suddenly I wanted to live — *really* live — experience something new; to face reality up close and feel it for a change.'

'So you bought an echoing manor house in the West Country and when you'd tamed all the spiders in there, you wondered what to do next?' There was a note of admiration in Sasha's voice.

'Something like that. I left my London life behind. Got all hands-on, back in touch with the earth's raw materials. Oak, granite, slate, marble.' His solemn look dissolved into laughter as he caught her eye. 'I got in touch with them, but then I didn't have a clue what to do with them.'

'I did wonder,' Sasha said as their laughter died down. 'You don't exactly look the type to — '

'Because I'm too cosseted and public-school to get my hands dirty? Would it surprise you to know that I'm the product of a comprehensive education? This expensive aura you detect around me is a figment of your imagination. I may lack manual skills, but I managed to build up my business without any hand-outs, and at least I have the decency to listen to what you have to say rather than jump to conclusions on the strength of a few superficial details which aren't even properly observed.'

Sasha froze at the insult. She snatched a glance at his profile, poised and fine as a marble statue. The smooth angles of his forehead, his nose and jaw were pleasingly balanced and his skin glowed with vitality; the length of his lashes sweeping downwards formed a dark fringe above his wide cheekbones; his firm mouth was generous and precisely defined.

She tore her eyes away before speaking. 'You're right. I'm sorry.'

'Have you ever been complimented on the speed and grace of your apology?' His tone was warm once more.

'It needs both when you've got a mouth like mine. Had plenty of practice,' she murmured, looking between her horse's ears. 'There's some faster riding when we get off the lanes, ending in a long gallop if you're up for it?'

'Sounds good to me.'

Coming onto the bridle path, Sasha took the lead and began to trot. Concentrating on her horse and the pace, she was glad to forget the complexities of conversation and work with her horse, a partnership she found far more simple. There was only the thudding of hooves, the crack of an occasional twig, her horse snorting, the creaking of her saddle. As they came through the gateway onto the hills she shortened her reins and leaned forward. Turning briefly to check that Seth was clear of the gate, she pressed her horse on, and slid her hands up his neck. The quickening of her pulse matched the speed of her horse and they raced forward into a gallop. She leaned against her horse's mane, feeling the warm vigour of his neck and glorying in the hectic pace.

Suddenly she was aware of Max, Seth's mount, racing beside her, riderless and wild, reins trailing perilously close to his legs. With a searing effort, she stretched out of her saddle and caught hold of the leather, just managing to retain her balance. Once back in the saddle, she got a firmer grip on the bolting horse and, with a combination of force and soothing words, slowed both horses down to a more controlled speed. At the top of the hill she came to a standstill, both horses snorting and hot. She turned to survey the wide view of the gallop, eyes scouring the hillocks and bushes for the shape of Seth. Nothing.

As she walked back down the hill, she remembered the panic she detected in Seth when his horse had spooked in the lane at the pheasant. It had been clear to her, at that moment, that Seth was not at home on a horse, and yet she had taken him on that gallop as a means of proving something to him. To show him that she might have the conversational subtlety of a sledgehammer, but she was a lot more sensitive than him in the saddle.

Taking both horses carefully down the furrowed track, she could still see no sign of him. She wondered whether to call his name in case he was stuck somewhere, unable to move, injured. The poor man had miraculously survived the car crash and moved here as a result — and now she had allowed him, even encouraged him, to participate in a ride far beyond his experience, and just for the benefit her own ego. And here he was, stranded somewhere — in pain, all alone . . . Sasha's imagination soared ahead.

'Seth . . . Seth — where are you?' She didn't want to shout because Seth's horse was still tense and sweating, but unless she bellowed, her voice sounded to her like a distressed croak. She carried on down the long descent, calling out his name, her voice becoming quieter as her fear intensified until she was merely whimpering, 'Seth, Seth, are you hurt?' Her throat burned and her eyes prickled but she gritted her teeth and blinked the tears back: this was no time for self-indulgence, she just had to find him.

'Seth . . . Seth . . . where are you?'

'If you look a little over to your right, just behind this very prickly bush — I know that, because I landed on it — you'll see me lounging on a rotten log. I see myself as a kind of adventure playground for woodlice.'

The voice was strong and cheerful.

'Seth! Seth . . . ' She breathed his name as she jumped off her horse, took off her hat, and made her way round the bush. Leaning against a mossy log, the odd twig clinging to his hair and a dark smear of mud across his bronzed face, reclined Seth. Eyes sparkling, brows arched, smile spreading; as if he were merely hosting a casual drinks party here on the hillock.

'You took your time,' he remarked. 'Is there something wrong?'

Sasha, overwhelmed with relief, choked out a sob and then gave her tears their freedom.

'Sasha, what's the matter? Are you hurt? Did something happen? Here.' He stood up, took off his coat and placed it back on the log before gesturing for Sasha to sit down. He crouched beside her, and put an arm round her shoulders as she sobbed into his chest. 'Sasha, stop. You're drowning me. Just tell me what's wrong.'

She moved her face up for air, twisting away from him, and took some deep gulps. 'I just thought I'd let you get hurt — after all you'd been through in London. When I couldn't see you, I started imagining you were badly injured.'

'Sasha, you are very lovely, but it's not your fault I'm a lousy rider. And if I'm so proud that I can't even admit how useless I am, then I fail to see how you are to blame.'

'But I could tell you were a novice — and I still took you on that gallop.'

'Serves me right, I'd have done the same to me! Especially after I forced you to apologise and then made you admit just how often you have to say you are sorry. Falling into a prickly bush is far too good for me. Here.' He took her face between his hands and moved the damp hair away from her watery eyes.

Sasha pulled a face and tried to look downwards.

'I'm not at my best with a swollen red nose and puffy eyes.'

'You look just fine to me. Beautiful, in fact. Sasha, please look at me.'

She forced her eyes upwards and, barely comprehending, took in the hunger of his expression. He pulled her forward until his mouth brushed gently against her own; the touch of his lips causing sparks to flicker deep within her, along with a rushing sensation in her ears.

Her mouth pressed into his — eager to taste him — and then, feeling a need to be closer still, she leaned into the warm hardness of his chest, feeling his heart pulsing against her own.

She was tugged back to her responsibilities by the reins on her wrist tightening as the horses tossed their heads and whinnied at an approaching group of ponies. Sasha was jolted back to the log on the hillock, and recalled the precarious balance of her relationship with Seth, not to mention her vulnerability, her dignity, her livelihood . . .

She leaped up, turned away, brushed herself down and, without a word to or a glance at Seth, began to busy herself with the horses.

4

'My idea was to get the indoor school laid out as close to this as we can manage, so we can partition a smaller area for disabled riding. What do you think?' Sasha fiddled with the large buttons of her red woollen coat, conscious that it was the first time Seth had seen her in anything other than her scruffiest riding clothes.

Since this was the first time they had gone anywhere together, she had decided to make an effort, even going so far as to elongate her brown eyes with smoky make-up and put on a few dabs of her favourite perfume. Now, standing close to Seth in the corner of the unfamiliar indoor school, she was aware of every inch of her body; unsure how best to hold her conspicuous limbs in clothes that were designed for real women, not stable-hands.

They were on a fact-finding mission, visiting a large stables in the next county. Sasha was determined that they should modernise their own business so they could start to offer riding for the disabled as well as beginners' lessons, and coaching for competition riders. If they could find ways to diversify, she was confident that their horses could begin to earn their keep.

'See, their square footage isn't any bigger than ours — they are just making all their space work,' she continued. 'Seth. Seth?'

The intensity of his gaze made her glance down to check that all the buttons of her top were done up, and then start twisting her charm bracelet anxiously round and round on her wrist. 'Seth, stop looking at me like that. What's wrong?'

'Sorry. Was just taking you in for a minute while you had your mind on other things and couldn't attack me. I was thinking it's a pity you don't make the effort more often. You're a beautiful woman — wasted on the horses, really, although I know they like you very much.'

He swerved away as she aimed a mock punch at his shoulder. 'And if that's what you're like when you're given a compliment, I'd hate to be around when someone insults you!'

She shook her head and assumed a stern expression. 'Right, if you've got all that smarmy stuff out of your system, perhaps you could concentrate on business for a minute. I'll try again. What do you think of the way they've laid out the school?'

'It's good. And a lot of the changes would be fairly superficial. The shell of our building is sound, so we can just work on the interior. What's next? Lead the way.'

'I wouldn't mind a quick look around the outdoor ménage before we grab something to eat; and then I can manage talking to the main disabled instructor on my own this afternoon, if you've got anything else you want to do.

I don't think it'll take too long.'

He stood back to let her out of the visitors' doorway and she walked ahead of him, uncomfortably aware of the visibility of her long legs. She walked stiffly across the space and leaned on the wooden fence of the exercise paddock, watching Seth cross the yard. The sun dappled his black hair and as he strolled across the concrete; seemingly unaware of his good looks, his face composed in a gentle smile as he approached her. She bit her lip until it hurt and then turned towards the paddock as he joined her.

'You riders are a formidable lot, aren't you?' he commented. 'Get a load of that man, he's heading this way, on that pale-coloured horse. He's got the snootiest expression on his face, really scary, and the horse is all covered in chains and straps — surprised the poor thing can move at all. Mind you, if I had him on my back, I'd want to get him off as soon as possible!' As he talked, Sasha's eyes roamed round the yard and came to rest on a horse and rider approaching from the left.

'Sasha — are you okay?' Seth enquired in concern as he took in Sasha's frozen stance.

'It's not — it can't be,' she whispered, clearly to herself. 'No — it can't be her. It is! It is!'

She moved slowly towards the horse and rider, oblivious to her surroundings and companion, as if sleepwalking. 'Jazzy . . . Jasmine.'

As she reached the golden horse, ignoring the rider, she stretched out her palm to the whiskery muzzle. The horse snorted, bit clinking, and then lowered blowing nostrils into Sasha's outstretched hand.

'It's you, isn't it? Hallo, Jazzy,' she soothed. 'I've missed you so much.' The horse visibly relaxed at the sound of Sasha's voice and the touch of her hand, sinking her head to rest softly on Sasha's shoulder.

'Get up, you,' were the first words spoken by the rider, causing Sasha to look upwards and see a man who was a match for the horse in terms of physical attributes. Dressed in full chaps, the suede accentuating the lean sinews of his legs, and a crisp cotton shirt, he gave the impression of an aristocrat playing at cowboys, but playing extremely well.

Eyes travelling upwards, she took in his skin, peach-coloured and with all the bloom of a ripened fruit; full, petulant lips, straight nose and almond-shaped dark eyes. His tawny blond hair was of a length to escape from the restraints of his skull cap, a few locks brushing his arched brows.

The man glanced at Sasha and then looked again with obvious interest. 'Have you come across this horse before, then? I'm trying to take her through the scales of training but she just doesn't want to know. She's fast and agile and pretty enough, but trying to get her to take things steady, get her hocks under, and balance — well, it just ain't easy and that's putting it mildly.

I've come here today to see if Gerry Pasternak, the instructor, has any suggestions — he's worked wonders with some of my problem cases in the past.' His voice was a casual drawl, but the emphasis on certain syllables suggested to Sasha that his neutral accent covered generations of good breeding.

The close presence of her beloved horse and clear approval of this superior being induced a hot simmering feeling in her stomach.

'She's Winter Jasmine, isn't she? You bought her from my aunt and she was actually my horse.' She spoke clearly and looked directly into his extravagant eyes — she wanted him to know just how significant she had been in his horse's past.

His eyes roamed over her body with more scrutiny than before as if sensing the need to re-evaluate his first impression. Sasha sucked in her stomach, generally observed her posture and tried to increase her stature. Something about his unabashed assessment made her feel excited and on display, as if she were a piece of horseflesh he was contemplating with cool detachment.

'Really,' he said at last. Sasha was squirming in the silence. 'I'm impressed. You've done a very fine job on the little mare, got her going well — taught her the rudiments. Now it's just the fine-tuning I'm having to work on.'

'I was interested in buying her back. I wondered how much you'd want for her?' said Sasha as the horse snorted and lowered her head back down to her caressing hand.

It was only when she heard Seth clear his throat that she remembered him. He was standing a little way back, hands on hips, watching the exchange through narrowed eyes.

'I can quite understand your concern for the horse — ' The rider paused as if searching for an appropriate endearment. 'I'm sorry, but I don't know your name.'

'Sasha.' She was still pulling herself

up taller, straighter, unusually aware of her stance.

'Sasha.' He caressed her name. 'I'm Guy, by the way. I can understand your concern for the horse, but don't you think that she deserves the best start to her competitive life? I feel a real empathy for this little mare and I'd like to take her to the top. Wouldn't you let her stay with me for while longer, so that I can make it all happen?' He phrased the question with husky-throated sincerity, as though it were something more than a rhetorical device.

As though hypnotised, Sasha found herself nodding. 'Yes . . . yes, of course I would.'

'How about I take your number and give you a bell sometime? Then, if you're interested, you could come over to my yard and give me a hand with her training.'

'That would be great — really great.' The words were stuttered and Sasha felt a vast smile splitting her face in two.

She leaned her face close to Jasmine's neck, aware that she was being watched by Seth and keen to compose herself.

'Well, what is it, then? Your phone number.'

Sasha was embarrassed to find Guy watching her, reins in one hand, mobile in the other. She gabbled out her number, astonished that she could remember it at all in the present company. And then Jasmine, gleaming like burnished gold, carried off her sublime rider into the distance, leaving Sasha speechless and adoring.

★ ★ ★

'Do you want to tell me about it?' asked Seth as Sasha sat in a world of her own, drink untouched, sandwich pushed aside, gazing into the middle distance and oblivious to Seth's company. 'Sasha?'

'Huh? Sorry.' She had been thinking about Jasmine, mainly about Jasmine, but also about her rider, and this gave her a guilty feeling as she blinked herself back to reality and acknowledged Seth. She gave a smile that reached no further than her lips while trying to push Guy's delectable eyes from her mind.

'The horse we saw? You haven't said a word since we left the yard,' he said gently. She realised with relief that Seth, as a distant spectator, hadn't noticed her fascination with the horse's owner.

'That's Winter Jasmine — the horse I was cross-questioning you about the first day I met you. Aunt Libby sold her the day before you made the offer for the yard. If only she had waited! She was my horse — Libby took her on as a foal. She was the subject of a cruelty prosecution brought by an animal charity, and she was confiscated from the owner.'

Sasha's features were animated with emotion and she leaned towards Seth. 'She was a complete wreck when we got her, but I fell in love with her. Who wouldn't? She's such a beauty. And it was magical to see her regaining her trust in people. By the end of the summer she was following me around like a dog — I'd feel her nose nudging me, asking for some more affection, and I brought her on very slowly and carefully. Last autumn, I finally put a bridle on her, and then the saddle — I thought we had all the time in the world together. But Aunt Libby was desperate for the money — end of story.'

She picked up her sandwich, nibbled at the crust and put it down. 'Anyway, let's stop now before I start sobbing all over you. I'm sure you could do without that.'

Seth's face was full of kindness. 'Look, I know you wish you still had her but at least she's not being starved or beaten. Perhaps stay in contact — your time will come.'

She nodded sadly. 'I know you're right, and anyway she's probably having a wonderful time with such a successful rider. Do you realise that was *the* Guy Palmer?' she said, without producing a noticeable reaction in Seth. 'He's a minor showjumper but he's more well-known as a TV presenter. He started off hosting some animal series on children's TV and now he does that cable programme — *Horsing Around?*' She raised her inflection at the end of sentence but Seth looked blank. 'Well, anyway, he's a bit of a celebrity and he was born in the saddle — so she couldn't have a better home.'

'Must have been uncomfortable for his mother,' observed Seth.

'Pardon?'

'Giving birth in the saddle.'

'Oh, shut up and listen.' Sasha shot him a glare and continued, 'I don't have the money to buy her back and I do know she's in good hands, but seeing her out of the blue — it was a bit like bumping into an old flame or a first love or something. Not that I've got much experience of that sort of thing.' She made an effort to laugh at herself.

'I don't believe that for a minute. You must have plenty of admirers — even if they never catch a glimpse of you without your riding clothes.'

'I didn't say I wasn't admired — although that sounds a bit grand for small-town dating — just that I'd never really put my heart and soul into a relationship.' Sasha found her eyes pulled towards his as if captivated, and her voice began to falter. 'Anyway, I'm not here to bare my soul about past loves, equine or human. How long do you think it would take to get the school transformed?'

'Hang on a minute, let me go down a gear. You're a great one for taking me on a conversational rollercoaster,' he said with the lightest touch on her bare arm. She immediately felt the heightened awareness of her body that his presence always generated, and had to look down at herself to check that her inner tumult was not visible in shaking hands or the magnified thumping of her heart. Then she set about trying to slide her arm away from his fingers without drawing attention to her actions.

'You're not the only one,' she muttered without thinking, the overwhelming thudding of her pulse momentarily confusing her.

'Glad it's not just me — I keep finding myself returning to those wonderful moments on the rotten log,' he murmured softly, keeping a light touch on her escaping arm.

'Don't. Forget it. It shouldn't have happened.' She pulled back her arm. 'I'm not one of those casual people, I can't just flit about, I'm not like you. I take things too seriously. We've got a good working relationship — let's hang on to that. It's important.' Her wide eyes were beseeching and she hugged her chest with both arms as she spoke.

He gave her a strange look, a brief smile, and nodded. 'Where were we? That's right, alterations to the school, how long? Simultaneous exchange and completion next Wednesday, and the builders are on stand-by. If they get on as well as they did on the house, they can break the back of the work in a couple of weeks.'

'And in that time we can buy the equipment, get on with tidying things up, book some advertising space and get going on the word-of-mouth stuff ready for a reopening with the local paper and perhaps a gymkhana or fun fancy dress riding or something, in a month — six weeks tops.' Sasha freed her arms to gesticulate as she spoke, but was careful to keep her hands clear of Seth.

'Sounds good to me,' he commented. 'and if you are bored in the meantime, you're welcome to help me organise my long overdue housewarming party. All my London friends are getting on my case about not having them down, and I'm running out of excuses.' He finished his drink, unwound his long limbs and slid out from the space behind the table with the casual grace of a big cat, before looking down at Sasha.

'Oh and by the way, you're invited — and before you start searching around for excuses, I won't take no for an answer.'

5

'No, I can't wear that. I know it's night-time but it shows everything,' Sasha protested as she wriggled frantically to let the red draped dress fall from her body onto the floor.

'You look fabulous in it!' protested her friend. 'Just fits you perfectly, like a glove.'

'But you know what I'm like. If there's too much of me on show I won't be able to move from the corner of the room all evening because I'll be so embarrassed. It might fit my figure but it's definitely totally unfit for my personality. And I've promised to go and give Seth a hand before the guests arrive, and there's no way I can help move tables and arrange glasses dressed in this. I'd die.' Sasha sat down on Anna's bed and took a gulp of tea. 'What next?'

'Something else that you'll refuse to wear.' Anna, getting ready to go out herself, was applying a sizzling red lipstick to her full lips. 'Why didn't you ask him how smart it was going to be? Would have made it all much simpler, you know.'

Sasha looked at her friend with pity reserved for the simple-minded. 'Because if I had, he'd know that it mattered to me how I looked tonight.'

'And so?' Her friend started to brush her long hair, still talking to Sasha's reflection in the mirror. 'Isn't it quite normal to care what you look like at a party?'

'Not if you're me. He knows I don't normally bother about all that fussy female stuff, and I don't want him to think that just because it's his party I'll act any different.' Sasha's eyes were fierce.

'But you are. I've never known you to get so worked up about clothes and make-up and hair.'

'Thanks for pointing that out,' Sasha said shortly, and started sifting through the swathes of dresses on the bed.

'Come on, Sash, you can tell me,' said her friend teasingly.

'There's nothing to tell. I just want to make a good impression, that's all. Lots of posh London people coming, I don't want to look like a country bumpkin. Now can we get on? Otherwise I'll be late. You must have something that I could wear without blushing.'

Anna nodded in satisfaction at her own reflection and turned to Sasha. 'I don't think I've got anything that doesn't show a bit of cleavage or leg.'

She stood with her hand on her forehead. 'Hang on a minute. I have got something. I bought it from that dress agency closing sale in Harley Didcott because it looked so beautiful on the dummy. It's just not right on me — where is it?' She shot over to her huge fitted wardrobe and began sifting through. 'Here.' As she brought out an short empire-line silk dress with full sleeves, it shimmered under the spotlight on the ceiling.

Sasha gasped. 'That is so beautiful.

Even I can appreciate it.' The lustrous material had a rich blue background printed with a dazzling array of large jewel-like butterflies: sapphire, emerald, ruby wings flew out of the midnight-blue background. 'Can I try it on?'

'No, Sash, I just want you to hold it for a while, perhaps stroke it and then put it away. Why do you think I'm showing it to you, dimwit? Get into it quick,' said her friend eagerly.

Sasha, sitting in just her underwear, stepped into the dress, pulling it over her long legs and slender body. Anna fastened the zip for her and then stood back.

'Well, madam, if you find anything wrong with this one, then you need your head examining and you can sort yourself out. Even you have got to agree that this looks stunning.'

Sasha, moving slowly to the mirror, could find nothing at all to say. Constantly in riding clothes or jeans, her current reflection suggested that an entirely different version of herself was possible. The dress complemented her tall, boyish figure but the beautiful cascade of exotic butterflies gave glamour to the simple lines of the dress.

Sasha pouted at her reflection and swished her the dress backwards and forwards, standing on tiptoes like a playing child, eager to dissipate the allure of the appearance.

'Right — now if we put your hair up . . . ' Anna sat her friend down on the bed and began to experiment with different styles. 'This is great, it's like having a Girls' World doll again.'

'I don't know why you didn't become a hairdresser rather than a cook.' Sasha winced as Anna tugged at her hair.

'Because I don't think I would have been very good at it,' Anna said cheerfully as she experimented with a french pleat, a look of happy concentration on her face.

'That inspires confidence,' Sasha said grimly.

'No, I'll be fine working on you. Whenever we go out anywhere, I'm always imagining what I'd do with you if I had a free rein. Your looks are so completely wasted on you.'

★ ★ ★

Prompt at seven o'clock, Sasha stood on the Manor House doorstep tugging her dress downwards against the breeze which threatened to expose her. She took the edge off her coral lip gloss with a tissue and jammed her feet harder into Anna's strappy sandals, the second highest pair on offer; she had balked at the highest. Feeling that no more could be done, but still horribly awkward, she tugged on the rusty chain bell pull and waited.

She could see Seth's silhouette through the glass panes in the door, moving closer and closer and she experienced a paralysing sensation of shyness. It was one thing meeting him at the stables — her territory — but in this unknown house of his, dressed up in clothes meant for a proper woman, helping to prepare for sophisticated London people, she was at a definite disadvantage.

'Hey, thanks for coming so early,' he said as he opened the door. 'I like the way you're always on time. Don't have a lot of patience for those types who always keep you waiting like they think they're worth it.' He was talking fast, as if he himself were nervous. 'I hope I've finally made the house respectable. After inviting everyone I know, I suddenly noticed hundreds of details that I'd completely overlooked, like a basin in the bathroom and a light in the hall and railings on the stairs. It's all fine for me — but then I don't mind camping.'

He was leading the way through the hall, still talking without stopping for breath. Finally reaching the end of the hall, he passed through a doorway into a huge and welcoming kitchen.

'I might as well tell you now how much I dislike parties, especially my own. I keep asking myself why I decided to have one.' He finally looked up at Sasha with a flickering smile and then gasped. 'Sasha, you look stunning. You really do.' He leaned close to her and brushed her cheek with his mouth. She froze, her heart pounding so forcefully she was afraid he would hear the effect his touch had upon her.

'Well, now I'm here, make use of me. What needs to be done first?' she croaked.

'Glasses. I picked up boxes and boxes of them today. And wine. The fridge is stuffed with white already. So if you can begin to unpack the red and the soft drinks — ? Then there's music. That high shelf up there is full of CDs that I've never bothered to unpack. And the food. I bought loads of stuff at the supermarket today and need to figure out quite what needs to be done with it all.' He paused, a smile slowly spreading over his tanned face until it caused his grey eyes to sparkle again. 'It's not exactly a high-end event, as you can tell.'

Sasha laughed. 'Still about the smartest thing I've ever been to. We do line dancing and cheese and wine round here, and that's as sophisticated as it gets.'

Seth's eyes lingered on her for a long moment and then he snapped back into action. 'I'll just get the boxes out of the hall and then we can get cracking.'

Sasha glanced up at the shelf containing the music. It was much too high for her to reach, but music would be more interesting to unpack than glasses; she was curious to discover Seth's taste. She looked around the room, found a tall stool in the corner and carried it to the far end of the kitchen, under the shelf. Delicately she climbed onto the high seat and began to stand, forgetting the extra handicap of Anna's second highest pair of strappy sandals.

'I've dragged in as many as I think we need. I've no idea how many people are coming, didn't want to calculate a grand total in case it made me feel worse — Sasha! What are you doing up there? Hold on, I'm coming . . . ' Seth put down the boxes and raced across the room, just in time to catch Sasha as she tumbled sideways into his arms.

'You complete idiot. How on earth did you think you'd be able to balance on there?' His voice relaxed into amusement as he caught an upside down view of Sasha's face, leaning backwards into his arms; the heels of her sandals teetering on the flagstones of the kitchen floor.

'Just trying to help,' she said, and watched his grey eyes move closer, so close that she could see the dark outline of the iris, and the flecks of green amongst the grey. She flung her head back so that their lips met and relaxed into his arms, letting him bear her weight. Sasha felt a delicious happiness run through her body; the warm glow overwhelmed her as her lips moved hungrily against his. And then, out of the blue, when she was weakest with a wonderful blend of desire and contentment, a small inner voice pierced her buoyancy, full of doubts as to his commitment, and her ability to fulfil all the high expectations he must have acquired through his increased age and experience.

She wriggled away, having to lunge forward and grab the edge of the table to avoid falling on her face as she writhed from his arms.

'Seth, this isn't right. I've told you. We come from different worlds, we want different things. I'm not the kind of person who can shrug things off, forget about kisses, pretend they never happened. I'm too serious — maybe it's something to do with the loss of my parents so young — I don't know. But that's the way I am.' She turned to catch his eye, tears welling up in her own. 'I can't help it. So don't mess about with me.'

Seth stood very straight, muscles taut in his neck and jaw, and looked past Sasha, hunched miserably at the table's edge, and out of the large window at the dusky view of the meadow below. He stayed there for a while, in silence.

When his shoulders had visibly relaxed he dropped his gaze down to the table height and walked towards Sasha. He touched her very lightly on the shoulder and she jumped.

'Sasha — I'm not the person you think I am. I don't know where you got the idea that I'm some urban playboy who'll toss you aside after I've had my wicked way. But that is what you're afraid, of, isn't it?' His voice was tender and concerned.

Sasha gulped back a sob and her croaky voice was barely audible.

'Why else would you bother with me? I haven't been anywhere, done anything exciting — even the dress I'm wearing tonight is borrowed. I don't even know how normal families behave — just my Aunt Libby, and then of course, the horses.'

Seth had to lean towards her buried face, folded into her arms, to catch her words. He crouched down next to her, close but not touching, and spoke softly in the direction of her hidden head.

'Sash, can't you see none of that matters? You're you; you're great, I admire you so much for your lack of self-pity about things, the way you just keep going. And you make me laugh and you're beautiful.

'And why would I care where you got that dress from? It couldn't look any lovelier on its owner than it does on you, and that's all that matters.'

Her head appeared slowly, her tears leaving streaks of make-up on her arms and great panda smudges on her face. She looked at him, her lips turned downwards in a pantomime expression of sadness, and then her mouth wobbled and her lips transformed into a smile.

'You're right. I don't know the first thing about you and I am very good at making assumptions. I've been good at doing that since the first moment I saw you. But if I'm to stop expecting the worst, perhaps I need to get to know you a bit more. And — ' she rubbed at her eyes with the back of her hand — 'my friend, Anna, would kill me. She

84

took ages with this make-up.'

They couldn't have crouched any closer to each other without embracing, their voices were soft, and their eyes drawn ever closer. They both started as the front door bell boomed into the kitchen. Seth looked round and then turned back to Sasha, his grey eyes boring into her as he spoke softly.

'I'd better get that. But don't dismiss what I said. I meant every word.'

6

For the first hour of the party, Sasha felt as if she was sleepwalking. As she introduced herself to each newcomer, and offered the mandatory amount of small talk, her mind was constantly returning to Seth's words. She could still hear his voice declaring his interest in her, and each time her mind repeated the phrases, she began to melt inside; actually having to lean against the side of the large fireplace at one point, as her legs threatened to subside into slush.

Meanwhile Seth was answering the constantly sounding front doorbell, greeting guests with the rich tones of a practised host, taking coats, fetching drinks, firing the jokes that inspired raucous laughter in each new guest, and making oblique references to people and events that Sasha could not share.

As Seth passed by, always going somewhere else, he touched her arm, smiled, always friendly but never intimate, before making another slanted reference to something beyond her sphere, causing her to feel ever more of an outsider.

And she was tired. She'd been working at the stable since six o'clock that morning, and after the stables, she had raced to Anna's house, making no time for food or relaxation. Now hearing the busy hum of strangers' conversation, interspersed with deafening laughter, in this unfamiliar house, all her doubts began to resurface.

'Here, is this yours?' asked a red-faced man as he returned from the drinks table with two tall flutes of sparkling white wine.

Sasha, who only drank occasionally, nodded gratefully, and took a large gulp of the fizzy liquid. The bubbles, as they burst against the top of her mouth, gave her a shot of energy and she began to sway gently to the background music that was playing, enjoying the sensation of the smooth silk of her dress as the butterflies danced in the soft light of the alcove where she stood.

The room was huge — two rooms, really. It ran the length of the house and was divided in the middle by two long folding wooden doors, drawn right back tonight. Sasha stood in her cosy alcove, feeling safe and hidden, and watched the guests, wondering how each of them had been connected with Seth's London life. That very willowy couple, man and woman, both crop-haired and dressed in fashionable masculine clothing, standing close and talking intently as if alone in the room. Was the London Seth a regular guest at their lavish dinner parties, or did they all visit the theatre together or even the opera? She didn't have a clue.

And those two hearty rugby types, both alarmingly red-faced. Voices roaring, simultaneously draining tall cans of beer and straight off to the drinks table again, eyes raking greedily over the bodies of all the women they passed. She couldn't imagine the Seth she knew having much in common with these two, but perhaps they were regular squash players or met at the gym; the three of them eyeing up the female members in their skimpy or figure-hugging clothes, giving them marks out of ten and then heading down the pub for more lewd conversation.

And that woman who was just entering the room — no, not entering: she was making an entrance. A long swaying stride, in heels that towered above Anna's highest pair, floating shot silk dress which shimmered like spun gold, cascades of buttery yellow hair. The throng parted in both directions to make way for her, and conversation stopped as guests, both male and female, snatched quick glances at her regal passage.

Sasha felt cold with fear at the thought of Seth interacting with this woman at any time, whether it was just a casual work friendship or even if she was merely the friend of a friend; any contact would be too close.

And now look at him, following in her wake trailing an armful of her possessions. Coat, scarf — and was that an overnight bag? Sasha watched him struggle with the separate items as he followed close behind the woman with an indulgent smile on his face.

As he passed by Sasha's alcove, for the first time there was no regard: not even a glance in her direction. Sasha picked up her champagne flute, stared through its bubbles at the inhabitants of the room, getting a pleasantly unreal fishbowl viewpoint, and then drained down its contents, scrunching up her eyes as the bubbles burned her mouth and tongue. She waited until Seth and his woman were clear of the drinks table and then came out of her alcove, for the first time that evening, to fill up her glass.

A young couple were doing the same. The smart woman with the bob held the glasses while the man poured from the bottle of red wine. When he had finished his task, the man with glasses gestured over to the door with his elbow.

'Seems like Karen's determined to work her magic again this evening.' He laughed.

'Hmmm. On one man in particular.' The woman raised her formidable eyebrows.

'Looks like she's already got him eating out of her hand. Did you see the way he was carrying her bags, fetching her a drink — 'it has to be a particularly sour martini with crushed ice and lime, not lemon'.' He mimicked a high lady's voice. 'And then she wanted 'a little freshen up and then to sit down somewhere a wee bit cooler and just catch up, it's been too long, Seth.'' He snorted. 'Seth? Well, he's just following orders.'

Sasha made a choking noise as she emptied her glass. Looking around for a refill, she found the heavy green bottle was empty and marched, nose in the air, to the kitchen where she knew more were stored in the fridge. She remembered stacking them there herself, when she was woozy with tenderness after the kiss, after the conversation, before Seth had started to display his strong attraction to all things London.

Already her head was swimming and she had to take exaggerated and precise footsteps to keep from tripping in her extra-high shoes. Judging herself the loser in a game that she could hardly bear to acknowledge she had been playing, she sat down under the coats and in amongst the boots and started unbuckling her sandals. Similar to the alcove, it was a cosy corner, smelling of leather and polish and dried mud: she breathed in her normal environment with relief and snuggled closer to Seth's boots.

'As I thought, however much he's tried to change his life, he can't run away from his feelings — he's completely besotted,' purred a female voice.

Sasha looked up and out through the

coats to see a French-polished hand belonging to a golden toned arm, joining onto what she could glimpse to be a shapely, glimmering torso. Karen, as her eavesdropping had revealed: former girlfriend to Seth.

'So what's your next move?' Another female voice.

'I've got to decide whether I want him back or if it's just the thrill of the chase. You know, now he's panting puppy-dog style outside my mansion block, whether I want to get him started on a whole new scent.' A musical laugh. 'Perhaps that new floral one by Hermès — or better still, Poison.'

'Oh, Karen. Stop joking around for once in your life.'

'Don't worry, I'm trying. I know that this is a man's life and future that I'm talking about and that I need to work out quite how much he means to me. Of course, I'm staying here tonight, and I can't decide whether to hole up in the spare room or perhaps do a little bit of bed-hopping once the other guests have left.' She gave a waterfall laugh. 'Perhaps I'll see how the evening progresses. The night is still young, after all.'

'I can't believe he's bought a riding stables. Seth, of all people,' the nameless woman said.

'I gave him a thorough grilling about that when we were on our own just now. Apparently, it was a spur of the moment thing, feeling heartbroken about me and making rash decisions. It's too late for him to undo the deal now but he says he's planning to get things running at a profit again and then sell up as a going concern. So all I need to do now — ' Sasha could hear the woman's lacquered fingernails drumming on the cracking plaster in the knothole somewhere above her head — 'is to decide if I want to be a part of his future, because without a doubt, he wants to be a part of mine.'

Only when the two voices were distant and then out of earshot, did Sasha move from the hiding place. She had a frostbitten feeling in her body, eyes too frozen to produce tears, although her teeth chattered if she didn't bite them together. In her stockinged feet, she made her way back to the kitchen, opened the fridge door and took out an icy bottle of sparkling wine. Leaning against the table, the scene of such earlier joy, she began to untwist the wire casing and tease out the entrenched cork ... She almost dropped the bottle as the cork broke free.

'Oi, are you trying to kill me?' yelled a gangly-looking man, around her own age, as the cork shot into his chest and bounced onto the floor. 'Here, you're losing it all.' He placed his glass under the cascade of bubbles overflowing the bottle. 'Where's your glass?'

She stretched out to take a clean glass from the stack on the table, more a tumbler than a flute, but since overhearing that conversation, she was beyond niceties.

When their glasses were full and the bottle placed between them on the table, the man began to talk. 'Hadn't imagined so many people would make it down tonight, but then he always was a popular man. Can't believe he's embarked on this crazy scheme to run a riding centre for the disabled. I mean it's all very worthy and everything, but it's not the kind of venture I associate with Seth. How long do you give it? Five minutes, three months?' The man was so tall that he had to bend his long neck down giraffe-like to address Sasha's face.

The alcoholic bubbles were thawing Sasha's frozen inner world, but not with a comfortable warmth — more a hot, prickly indignation.

'Since I happen to be the main worker on this new scheme, it would be nice to think that it was a considered business plan rather than a hare-brained way of escaping from London life,' she retorted.

She could see angry red patches covering the man's face as he took in her words. He stammered, 'I'm so sorry. I had no idea. Just goes to show that you should watch your mouth at these sort of events — you never know who you are talking to. I don't know what I'm talking about, quite honestly, just heard a lot of gossip tonight about sixth-hand from other people who probably haven't got a clue either.'

She patted his arm. 'It doesn't matter, I'm honestly not offended.' She started to move away.

'Here, can I top you up?' He gestured to her glass with the bottle. 'I vote we keep this one to ourselves. It's quite a good one, and there's only the cheap stuff left in the fridge now.'

'Whatever you say.' Sasha had plans to leave as soon as she could gather up her dignity and address Seth without the risk of tears or anger, but in the meantime she took another swig.

★ ★ ★

When Sasha announced to the gangly man that she was leaving, she still couldn't remember his name, although they had been jokingly intimate for the last half hour or so. She slipped off her perch on the table's edge and found that she could no longer rely on the stability of her own two feet, even without those ridiculous shoes.

'Steady on,' said the man. 'How far do you need to go?'

'Only down the drive to the stable.' Sasha over-enunciated, aware of the potential for slurring her speech. 'It's quicker across the fields, but I don't think I'm fit for cross country at this time of night.'

'Here, lean on me. It's been great to share a bottle of champagne with you, but you look like you'd find a ten-minute stroll down the drive a bit of a challenge right now.' He put his arm round her as she slumped against his shoulder. 'I'm staying at the bed and breakfast in the village. I'm about ready to get going myself. If you hang on here, I'll go and find Seth and get him to ring me a cab, then I can give you a lift back to the stables.'

He pushed her gently down onto a low chair in the corner and she sat and watched the guests, in triplicate, as she waited for the gangly nameless man to return.

* * *

'It's here now, come on.' He startled her out of her daze, and she allowed herself to be pulled up from the chair by the arm and led across the room.

'Sasha!' She heard Seth's voice as she stumbled through the hall. 'Are you okay?'

'Just a bit the worse the wear from sparkling wine,' the man answered for her, in condescending tones, from somewhere above her head.

'I thought you didn't drink.' Seth's sculpted face loomed so close to her own that her eyes lost focus completely.

'I don't,' she said and recoiled as the full force of her emotional hurt hit her through the alcohol. 'Come on, darling.'

She managed to raise her face somewhere in the general direction of her lanky companion. 'Let's get straight in that cab.' She aimed a kiss as high up as she imagined him to be. 'I can't wait to get you home.'

7

The morning after the night before, Sasha's first sensation on waking was throbbing feet. She cast her mind back and, even under the cover of the duvet, winced, closed her eyes tight shut, and curled into a ball. The loss of Anna's second highest heels was easier to contemplate than her own behaviour and so she shuddered about their casual treatment for as long as she could; how could she have abandoned them at the party? They belonged to her best friend since childhood. Anna would kill her. She hoped the dress was still intact, and then as her hands checked over her body, she discovered she was still wearing it.

Her head felt bruised and slow, even as she rested on the bed. The night before came back as a jagged series of freeze frames, replayed from the indignity of the taxi home at the end of the night, through to the breezy hopefulness of Seth's arms at its beginning. She shuddered, and discovered that the slightest movement caused shockwaves to reverberate throughout her skull.

The horses! She dragged her head out from under the clammy duvet and peered at the illuminated display on her clock. She had slept through her alarm by nearly two hours and the poor hungry horses had no one else to feed them. She was working singlehanded at the stables, seven days a week, until a suitable assistant could be found. She had assured Seth that she was used to the work, enjoyed it even, and refused Libby's offer to stay on and help for the time being. No, she had forced Libby to stop work there and then — and, at this moment, Libby was enjoying an off-season deal at a luxury hotel in Dorset.

★ ★ ★

Sasha was a bit patchy on astrophysics but by the strength of the sun's brilliance, Sasha would hazard a guess that it had moved several thousand light years closer to earth since yesterday. She had to squint and then close her eyes completely, unable to face its dazzling scrutiny. After a couple of tries, she gave in and shouldered her way into the kitchen to scrabble in the miscellaneous drawer for a pair of sunglasses. All she could find was a crooked pair with one broken arm that had belonged to her almost a decade ago. Hoping for a number of reasons that she wouldn't bump into anyone, namely Seth, she tried the outside world once again.

She grabbed an armful of head collars, filled a bucket with pony nuts and, holding her head as still as she could, made her way to the first meadow where the small ponies were turned out. Mechanically, she allowed the first two to approach her, whiskery noses plunged into the feed bucket, caught them and led them across the yard. On automatic pilot, she repeated the process until all the hardy ponies were tied up in stalls, munching on their hay nets. She hobbled on her bruised feet to the loose boxes where the horses were kept and began to feed and water them, telling herself she was nearly there and having to mutter encouragements to complete a job that she had done almost every day for the last ten years.

When the last horse was fed, she leaned out of the shelter of his box, hearing the contented munching of horses eating all over the yard. The icy pain and hot anger of last night had settled into a heavy sadness, lodged somewhere within her chest. While she busied herself with the needs of the horses she could avoid facing the cause of her pain.

Seth would be down later — that was, if he could tear himself away from that woman and the gossip of his real friends. Unable to face seeing him, she locked the feed room, closed the gate into the yard, and hurried back into the cottage.

After an hour of intense deliberation, during which she sat on the bottom step of the cottage's twisted staircase, she had to accept that she could no longer work with Seth. She might be hard on herself but she was no masochist, and the idea of continuing contact with the man who had encouraged her to believe in fairytale endings was too painful to contemplate. She must find a fresh beginning for herself, and as quickly as possible. She had endless skills and experience, and if she started now she was sure that by the end of the day she would have found herself a new position at another stables, however lowly.

Local directory in front of her, open at Riding Stables, she worked her way through this list, explaining that her present position was no longer tenable, and requesting a chance to prove herself even for a cut in salary. But it was Sunday morning, not the best day for job hunting, and her polite queries received flat refusals at each of the stables she contacted. Head buried in her hands on her lap, the most comfortable position she had found for herself today, outside the cover of her duvet, her mind turned to Winter Jasmine, and the horse's new owner.

Guy Palmer had definitely offered her the opportunity to visit his stables and help in Jasmine's schooling. He might not have meant it (although his lustrous eyes had widened in sincerity, she now recalled), but she was desperate and it had to be worth a try. The only problem was that for all his candour, he had neglected to give her his phone number. Sasha sighed and slumped further, actually sliding down to the next step in her despondency. She tried to summon up another escape route but her head had stuck at Guy Palmer's yard. If she was forced, through Seth's behaviour, to leave her lifelong home, it felt fitting to be moving to her former horse's new territory.

His contact details had to be around

here somewhere. He was a well known figure in the horse world, holding training days, rider boot camps and giving after dinner talks; he was hardly going to hide his whereabouts if he wanted the business. And wasn't this cottage, although short on many of the creature comforts other people took for granted, home to an entire collection of Horse and Hound magazines dating from just after the beginning of the space race? What would have been the spare room was home to sheaves of yellowed pages; at least her research would only make use of the small pile closest to the door.

The last year's magazines under her arm, Sasha positioned herself business-like at her aunt's desk, refreshingly clear of paperwork now the sale of the stables had gone through. She flicked through endless articles and classified ads until, in the first magazine she opened, she came upon Guy Palmer, a posed photo of his profile next to a long-maned horse and the contact details she was after, laid out in bold type.

Before she had time to think, she reached for the phone on the desk and typed in the number. For the few rings she tried to arrange a wide smile on her face, having heard that it would make her voice sound positive, and then the deflating sound of the answering machine.

Because it was Guy Palmer's own voice, sounding remarkably accessible and friendly, despite his celebrity status, Sasha found herself leaving a message.

'Hi, I don't know if you remember me, I met you at Harcourt Stables about three weeks ago. My name is Sasha and I used to own your horse, Winter Jasmine. At the time you said it might be possible to participate in her training, and now I'm between jobs — actually looking very hard for a new one, things aren't working out at the present yard — it's been taken over by a new boss and we don't see eye to eye.

'Anyway, I don't know why I'm telling you all this but what I mean is

I'd love the opportunity to work with you, that's all and I'm not afraid of hard work.' And then she left her number, muttered a bit more information he didn't need to know in stuttering tones, tried to understand her aunt's answering machine by turning it on and then pressing and depressing a lot of buttons, wished she had left a more sophisticated message and settled down, head on folded arms on her aunt's desk.

★　★　★

She was close to sleep when the door banged. Not sure if she had imagined the noise, she waited until the knock was repeated before forcing herself to open the door. Seth dominated the tiny doorway, unshaven, rumpled and lamentably handsome.

'I need to talk to you — is this a good time?'

'Not great, but you can come in.' She filled up the kettle and busied herself washing up two mugs that were already clean and searching out a new box of teabags when there was a full tin sitting on prominent display beside the kettle.

'Did you enjoy last night?' Seth's voice was grim.

'What do you think?' She began pouring more sugar into an almost full bowl.

'That I was surprised and hurt by your sudden attraction to that young lad, Simon. Nice though he is, I thought the conversation we had earlier actually meant something to you. More fool me.' He spat out the last three words.

'Yes, I thought so too.' Her voice was quiet, but she enunciated the words clearly.

'Then what went wrong?'

'You and your London friends.' She refused to turn in his direction.

'My friends? You certainly seemed to be getting on a little too well with one of them.'

'I could say the same for you.' Her voice was clipped and she blinked back the tears that once again threatened her eyes.

'What are you talking about?' he roared. 'Can you just drop all that cleaning and tea-making and turn around and face me and explain yourself? One minute we were in each other's arms, promising commitment, and the next, you develop a furious thirst and slope off in the arms of some awkward adolescent, gearing up for a night of passion.'

Sasha could hear his footsteps as he moved round the table to stand behind her, but she still refused to look at him. She could feel his presence, see his shadow darkening the worktop, smell his delicious scent of warm citrus mingled with fresh sweat. The longer she avoided his eyes, the harder she found it to abandon her stance and face him.

'Yes, there was the happiness and the promise and the hope, and yes, I did leave at the end of the night in an embarrassing state of drunkenness with a man who held no interest for me other than as a useful support. But you missed something out of the sequence: your part, what you did.' Her voice was quiet but harsh with the pain it contained.

'My part? You're not making any sense at all.'

She felt his hands on her shoulders and he pulled her round to face him. She swung without any resistance, like a doll, but her eyes were downcast. 'I'm not blind and I'm not stupid and I'm certainly not deaf,' she muttered.

'I have to agree that you are none of those things, but you certainly are very difficult to understand.' There was less anger in his voice now.

'You threw me into a room with all your London friends and all their gossip and then you ignored me, preferring a certain lady from your past. What's she called? Karen, isn't it? Her name was on everyone's lips — that is, when they weren't discussing quite how mad you were to take on this crummy stables in the country and speculating about just how long you'd last.' She looked up at him, her eyes blazing.

'Yes, her name is Karen. And she was one of the main reasons I had begun to dread the party — the idea of seeing her again.'

'Because it would bring it all back, all the heartbreak she'd put you through?' she said to the floor.

'I beg your pardon? Heartbreak wasn't an issue. Remember, I broke it off with her.' He sounded confused.

'Then why didn't you want to see her?'

'Because I'd realised how much simpler and more pleasurable life was without her constant game-playing; I didn't miss her at all. But I knew that an evening with her would not be complete without some sort of agenda. She's not nasty, it's just the way she enjoys herself, a strange sort of hobby.' He laughed without humour.

'I heard some of your friends talking, I heard her talking, I saw you dancing attendance. I jumped to the obvious conclusion.' Her voice was high with indignation.

'And you didn't trust me?'

'And did you trust me?' She looked up at him and their eyes locked in an exchange of mutual accusation. As her eyes continued to stare unblinking, her mind sifted through his behaviour, considering the possibility of his innocence.

After a long pause, she moved her hand onto his arm. 'I didn't do anything. I said goodbye to whatever that man was called at the entrance to the stables and stumbled into the house on my own, and nothing went on in the taxi — in fact I was in the front seat beside the driver, trying very hard not to be sick. I just wanted to hurt you, and being unused to the effects of alcohol, the way I chose to do it might not have been particularly subtle.'

He took hold of her hand. 'Might not have been subtle, but it was still successful. I didn't sleep last night, I was too busy tossing and turning and leaping out of bed and pacing the room and muttering to myself and working my way through the evening trying to understand why you had pretended to care for me, and what Simon had done to make you change your mind.'

'And Karen wasn't keeping you company?'

He grinned. 'I have no idea what Karen was doing. She was the furthest thing from my mind as I screwed up the sheet and thumped the pillow and groaned with frustration and misery and longing. Does that answer your question?'

They fell into each other's arms. As they stood unmoving and silent, her head on his chest, Sasha luxuriated in the renewal of hope. Anything that life could throw at her — even the pain of the distant past — seemed infinitely more bearable while she was enfolded in Seth's firm grasp.

And then the phone rang on her aunt's desk. Just one ring and then it clicked onto the answering machine. As she cast back her mind to just half an hour earlier, she discovered that her experimental button-pressing had caused the message to play out the message at high volume. She unfolded herself from Seth's arms and took a step back.

'Hi,' drawled the voice, syllables even longer on the phone than they had been in person. 'It's Guy here, just returning your call, Sasha. Of course I remember you. How would I forget your chocolate-coloured eyes and your stunning bone structure? I'm sorry your new boss is giving you a hard time — one of those little-Hitler types, is he, who wants to march on in and change everything? As far as you giving me a hand with Jasmine and taking on a full time position at the yard — I have to say I'm very interested. Give me a call later, I'm in the house for the rest of the afternoon, and I know we can work something out. Bye then, Sasha.'

His voice grew husky on the last sentence and slipped into a tender whisper as he said goodbye.

Sasha gritted her teeth, took a large breath and commanded her unwilling eyes to look at Seth. 'It's not what you think — it's not how it sounds at all.'

'Really. I'll be interested to see how you can take the sting out of that message. Go on then, have a go,' he challenged, and she could hear the hurt catching on his words, even though his tone was icy cold.

'This morning, I was in a right old state, like you. I was convinced that you had been stringing me along, making a fool of me and all the time carrying on with Karen. And so I decided — bear in mind I also had the first hangover I've ever had in my life, and it made my mood more despairing — that it would be impossible for me to work with you any more.' She looked up at him, her wide eyes imploring him to understand. He glared back.

'So I just worked my way through all the stables in the local directory. I didn't care about their reputations or how junior the job might be, I just needed something away from here.'

'So you felt the need to tell all these people about your unreasonable boss, did you?'

'No, actually, I didn't. I just rang them, told them my experience and asked if they had any vacancies and they all said no. So then I remembered meeting Guy — you were there that day. And how he'd said he'd love me to come and help him with Jasmine. Do you remember?' she pleaded.

'Yes, of course I do.' His lips were thin with tension.

'So I found his number and rang him up because I thought that if I had to leave my home, then the next best thing would be to move to my horse's new home, and so I left a message for Guy. And I may have rambled on a bit because I'm not very good on the answerphone — but at least I didn't tell him that you had broken my heart and that I didn't know where I stood with you in terms of commitment. I could hardly say that in a message and of course it's not something I'd want to tell him anyway, so I just said that I'd found I couldn't get on with you and he drew his own conclusions.' She managed the whole explanation without pausing for breath, scared that he would interrupt with his own interpretation.

'And I suppose you banked on the fact that he'd remember your chocolate-brown eyes?' There was a sneer in his voice that she had never heard before.

'Of course not — it was the horse I was — ' She could hear her voice rising into a high pitched squeal.

Seth held his hand up to silence her. 'Don't. I don't want to hear any more of your excuses. 'Oh Seth, I'm a serious person,'' he mimicked her. ''Oh, Seth, I'm not the kind of person who can shrug things off.'' He glared at her. 'Unless it's for a handsome — if you like that kind of thing — minor celebrity and a horse who seems to mean more to you than any person ever could.'

'Seth, it's nothing to do with Guy — or even Jasmine, really. I told you that I rang around all the other stables first!' Her anguished shriek actually hurt her own ears.

'Ah, but I've only your word for that — just like I've only your word for what happened with that adolescent with the overgrown Adam's apple who you picked up last night. I'm beginning to think that you are not what you seem.'

Hearing Seth speak in these contemptuous tones caused her real pain — she could feel a stabbing sensation somewhere in her chest, perhaps where her heart lay.

'Seth, how can you talk like this? It was because of what happened last night that I rang round — I truly thought you were back with *her*. I don't want to go — not now that we've sorted out how we really feel about one another.'

She moved towards him, her arms outstretched, but he just brushed her away.

'Have we?' His skin was pulled taut over his cheekbones and she noticed the shadows under his eyes. His hand reached for the latch on the front door and he hesitated. 'There'll be plenty of time to discuss working out your notice and the other practical details another time.'

8

Sasha retreated to the staircase once more and sat hugging her knees and trying to still her lurching heart. She listened to the noises of the cottage: the creak of the floorboards and the rattling of the rafters, and then moved on to the sounds of the yard. One horse, probably Toby, was banging on the stable door with his hooves and another horse, Rosie, was whinnying in the nearest meadow, and she could hear the cheeping of young birds and the cawing of crows and the roar of distant cars on the main road. She forced herself to isolate more sounds in an effort to distract herself from the confusion of her thoughts.

She was doing a fairly good job, actually finding rhythms and harmonies in the various noises, when her restless mind returned to Seth's scornful tone of voice as he had accused her of lying to him. The voice and words echoed in her head and aroused her emotions until all other thoughts were sidelined. How could he think these things of her? She had to make him understand how wrong he was.

Without pausing to think, she grabbed her jacket from the back of a chair, left the cottage and marched up the drive to the Manor House.

As she stood on the doorstep at about the same time as she had done yesterday, she realised that she hadn't caught sight of herself in a mirror at all that day, nor had she combed her hair. She checked her jeans and found the bottoms encrusted with mud. Her jacket had a large rip on the shoulder where she had caught it on barbed wire the day before yesterday. As she pulled the chain of the bell, it occurred to her that perhaps she should have made a little more effort with her appearance.

I'm too used to socialising with horses, that's my problem. Perhaps I should have asked one of them to lend me a mane comb at the very least, she thought wryly. She tugged at her hair as the door swung open.

It was the long expanse of bare leg that first caught Sasha's attention. The woman who answered the door was wearing a raw silk robe in a breathtaking shade of violet which stopped at the very upper limit of mid-thigh. At this point the endless, shapely legs took over the decorative role, finishing in a surprisingly small pair of narrow feet, pink and soft as a child's, steady and at home on Seth's flagstones.

Sasha felt her stomach churning at the sight of Seth's ex-girlfriend. *Don't jump to conclusions*, she told herself firmly. *It's what we both keep doing and that's why we're in this mess.* She took a deep breath, pulled herself up to her full height and faced Karen.

'Hi. If you're looking for Seth, he's not in. He's just popped out to fetch us a takeaway — at my insistence — said I was so hungry I could eat a horse, although I appreciate the remark is in rather poor taste round here.' Karen's distinctive cascading laugh jarred on Sasha's ears. 'You're welcome to wait. I could do with a bit of company. It's far too quiet round here — unnervingly so, actually.'

She didn't wait for Sasha to reply, just opened the door wider and gestured her inside with a soft white arm. 'No, Seth was going to feed me some rustic speciality — organic ham and crusty loaf and finest sheeps' cheese from the region, but I just rebelled. Absolutely insisted that I needed some E-numbers right this minute or my body would go into shock. No wonder he's gone a bit strange — this environment is hardly what he's used to.'

'Oh, I don't know. He seems to be coping fairly well as far as I can see. Pulls his weight at the stables.' Sasha forced herself to respond, although she was inwardly recoiling from the woman's presence. *She's just playing games, like Seth says she does,* Sasha tried to reassure herself against her gathering doubts.

'Is that where you come from?' Karen gave a generous smile revealing alarmingly straight and small teeth.

'Do you mean, did I crawl out of the hay barn? I know I look a bit like that at the moment — sorry for my scruffy appearance, it's been a long, hard day. But I do actually live in a real house — made for human beings, not four legged creatures!' Sasha tried to inject some humour into her laugh, but it sounded false in her ears.

'Oh, please don't apologise to me. I'm hardly in a fit state to entertain. Sorry — I wasn't expecting visitors.' Karen glanced down at the long view of her body, making her butter-yellow hair swing over her shoulder and ripple down her side like a mermaid. 'It's not that I didn't love last night, but entertaining large groups is all very formal, don't you think?'

Sasha had no idea what she thought but found herself agreeing. 'Yes, definitely.' She even nodded to increase the emphasis.

'And so I always feel it's important to strike a balance and unwind the next day. Hence the dressed-down state. Seth wanted to take me out and show me around — I think he wanted me to get dressed up to the nines so he could show me off to the area.' She gave a peal of laughter. Sasha wondered if they had laughing lessons in London. 'But I insisted. 'Seth,' I said, 'you know the rules; if we go public one night, then the next we just hang out *au naturelle*.''

I thought Seth wanted her to eat rustic bread and organic ham, thought Sasha, before finding herself nodding again, puppet-like. The woman seemed to have a hypnotic effect on her social manner.

'Can I get you anything?' Karen led the way into the living room, not waiting for an answer, and positioned herself on the only sofa, making full use of its length as she reclined on it as though it were a chaise longue.

Any minute now she'll have me peeling her grapes, thought Sasha. She moved to stand in the same alcove she had haunted the previous night, unwilling to settle anywhere in the room.

'Do you think Seth will be long?' she asked.

'No idea. I told him to drive like the wind itself, but I wanted Thai food and he said he'd probably have to cross two counties to find that. I said, 'So be it, surprise me then.'' She licked her wide mouth with a small perfect pink tongue, like a Siamese cat.

Mind you, everything about her's perfect, thought Sasha, *she's like another species, I couldn't begin to compete.*

'Well, he's probably rowing over the first river at this moment — and then there will be the mountain to climb, and after that he'll be killing that dragon that guards the Thai takeaway shop,' Sasha joked in an attempt to relieve the tension. She braced herself for Karen's laugh but this time it sounded a little more strained.

'You're Sarah from the stables, aren't

you?' she said after a silence.

'Sasha — but yes, I'm from the stables.'

'Seth said that you've been practically brought up by the horses,' Karen remarked.

'By my aunt, actually, but she's half-horse, I think, so you're not very far wrong.' Sasha found herself edging even closer to hysteria.

'Seth says you are a real find, an asset for the stables, someone who gets on better with animals than with people. He thinks it'll be good for the stables if he can persuade you to stay in the background out of the way while he takes over the people skills that you are lacking — he was explaining it all to me earlier.'

She gave a long feline stretch. Sasha could imagine her purring.

'Was he.' It was not a question.

'Yes, we were talking a lot about the stables, actually. The organisation of the business, allocation of roles.' She paused for a moment letting her words hang in the quiet. 'I will still spend a fair amount of time in London at first until I can build up a consultancy role, which will be less hands-on, but it all takes time.'

Sasha gained control of her dropping jaw and made it speak.

'You're moving here?'

'Of course. It's all very sudden and I don't suppose Seth thought it a priority to tell you, he's been too busy phoning around our friends. Of course they are all thrilled. I think a lot of them were hoping that the party would achieve this kind of result — make us both see sense, you know.'

Sasha felt the last remnants of conviction desert her. Instead an uncomfortably large lump stuck into her throat. She gulped it down where it settled, painfully, somewhere close to her heart. Having nothing to say, she just looked down at her scruffy trainers.

'All our friends, they've been driving me mad and Seth says they've been doing the same to him. They won't talk about anything else except what a huge mistake we're making. How we are made for each other — it's obvious to everyone — and can't we just swallow our stupid pride and kiss and make up?' Karen's smile widened and her eyebrows arched. 'So that's just what we did — at great length — last night.'

Sasha still said nothing. She felt as if she was in one of those 'trapped' dreams, the kind she had always had as a child, where her legs wouldn't work and her voice wouldn't work, but she desperately needed to shout for help or escape. She wanted to force herself to make some excuse and leave but her conversational ability appeared to have left the sinking ship at the same time as her get up and go.

She heard the crunch of the front door closing and didn't feel relieved. Not only would she now have to face Seth, but, if she wanted to keep her pride intact, she would actually have to congratulate him on his romantic good fortune.

She still focused on her trainers but, out of the corner of her eye, could see Karen arranging herself on the sofa.

'I'm afraid spare ribs and a few spring rolls was the best I could do. Hardly your style, I know, but I wasn't prepared.' Seth's voice entered the room first. 'And I'm warning you now that if you start complaining about the quality of the cooking, I'm going to chuck you out on the drive and you can find your own way home, flat battery or not.'

At the sound of Seth's voice Sasha had to look upwards. He looked tired, disgruntled and heart-stoppingly attractive.

'Seth,' she said bravely. 'I was going to have a quick word, but having been updated on the situation by Karen, I don't think it will be necessary.'

'I dread to think what Karen would need to update you about.' He gave a lopsided smile. 'Can we talk things over later? I think I might have misjudged the situation — ' he paused and pulled a pitiful face — 'for a change.' He nodded in Karen's direction.

'When I got back from seeing you, I found Karen limping up the drive. Apparently her battery had become inexplicably flat a few minutes down the road and she thought it best to base herself here. Chiefly so that she could have me running every errand imaginable — isn't that right, Karen?' He grinned wryly.

'Oh, Seth, you don't need to concoct any more of your tall tales for Sarah's benefit.' Karen slipped her legs off the sofa and sat up in one graceful swoop. 'Yes, we've really become quite good friends while you've been out, Sarah and I. In fact I've let her in on our little secret.'

'You have?' Seth looked confused. 'And who is this Sarah? I know Sasha here — very well — but I've yet to meet a Sarah.'

'Sasha, yes.' Karen waved her hand as if names were a mere irrelevance. 'We've done some talking and I thought it was about time she knew about our plans for the future.' She gave a wink that she somehow managed to make look sexy, and then threw back her head and let out her musical laugh.

Seth groaned. 'I have no idea what you have said to Sasha but I can make a pretty good guess.'

'Oh, Seth, don't be such an old stick in the mud. Sasha needs to know about us at some point, although I'm still waiting for some form of congratulation from her.' She shook out her long hair, pulled a file out of her pocket and began to buff her nails.

'Karen, you are quite unbelievable.' Seth rolled his eyes. 'I may well chuck you out before you've even had a chance to taste this takeaway.' He turned to Sasha. 'You know what I told you about Karen's advanced level game playing with people's lives — kind of seeing how far she can push it. Is it a kind of thrill-seeking, Karen? Perhaps you should take up hang-gliding or free-falling.'

'A bit too cold for my liking. And dirty, too,' Karen remarked without looking up from her nails.

Sasha turned her head to and fro, watching the exchange like a game of ping-pong. She felt confused and exhausted; she suddenly longed to be back in her cottage, preferably with Aunt Libby, chatting about the horses as they ate something cosy, like soup.

The homeliness of the imagined scene brought tears to her eyes.

'Right, I think I'll be off.' She made for the door. 'I can see you've got a lot to talk about.'

Seth reached out to touch Sasha's hand. 'Sasha, don't go like this.'

There was a clear note of anxiety in his voice which unnerved Sasha. Seth's confidence was a quality she had come to rely upon.

'Seth, I feel totally confused. One minute you're accusing me of lying, the next I hear how you're blissfully happy with Karen.' Her head still ached from the night before and the twists and turns of the day seemed to have reduced her bewildered mind to a standstill.

'That's Seth all over.' Karen was leaning forward to listen to the muttered conversation and she looked at Sasha with sympathy. 'He's a really nice man, acts from the highest of motives but you never have a clue where you stand with him, and then he tries to tell you that you're playing games and that he's been strong and steady all along.' She gave a mock frown and shook her head slowly. 'Get used to it. That's what I say. I've known him long enough — and he's not going to change now.'

'Karen. Can you just stay out of this and manage to keep your mouth shut, just for a little while? What you are doing here is simply not funny,' growled Seth.

'Oh turn it back on to me again when I'm just trying to give the poor girl a little bit of advice. She could do with some, by the look of her.'

Sasha felt a tear plop onto her hand, another trickle down her cheek, but she was too tired for proper crying. She let the tears fall without brushing them away. It felt right to let Seth and Karen observe the raw misery of her state; maybe then they'd feel more inclined to let her in on the truth of their world. The last few days with Seth had been like living in one of those halls of contorted mirrors — so many versions of life on offer that she had no idea where reality lay any more.

Seth's grey eyes appeared soft with understanding and, seeing her tears, he reached a hand forward to touch her arm. Sasha backed away. She didn't want to get any more involved — since Seth Marston had bought up the stables, life had got far too complicated. Emotions had been stirred that were better left dormant, and now she needed to escape all these uncomfortable feelings.

'I don't know what's going on between you two, and it's none of my business anyway. I just hope you can make each other very happy. I've decided that it would be easier for both of us if I left the stables. I'll let you know how I get on.'

9

Before Sasha had even finished parking her battered car, Guy Palmer was waiting for her at the five-barred gate into the yard. He had a fond expression in his shining eyes, the floppy blond hair hanging over his forehead accentuating his youthful good looks. When Sasha got out of the car, awkward and self-conscious under his scrutiny, he greeted her like a long-lost friend.

'Sasha — you don't know how happy it made me when you rang. I'd actually been thinking of you the last few days, wondering if you meant what you said about wanting to help me. And then when you got in touch yourself, it was like a kind of destiny, wasn't it?' His eyes were bewitching. 'Although I don't really believe in all that nonsense, of course,' he finished quickly.

'Of course I meant it. I'd love to

work with someone of your experience and to help with Jasmine's training — well, it would be a bit of a dream come true. You should have rung me earlier.' She found that she was having to reassure him. Her, reassuring Guy Palmer — imagine!

'Didn't know whether you'd be pleased to hear from me,' he said quickly, and looked down at his feet.

Sasha raced to his defence. 'Guy, you're such a huge success. I would have been bowled over, I was actually close to swooning when you rang me back.' His open, confiding manner had put her at her ease immediately. She felt as if she could be herself with him — as though they would be bound more closely by their insecurities.

He shrugged and opened the gate. 'Do you want to have a look around the place — see if you think you could fit in here?'

'Gosh, yes.' She followed him through the gate.

The yard was of an entirely different

calibre to the one she had just left. A huge American-style barn housed his horses, all facing outwards onto a covered central space. The buildings were constructed from a caramel-coloured wood that toned with Guy's hair.

'Do you like?' he asked, taking in her awed expression.

'Oh, it's wonderful. A million miles away from the stables I'm used to.'

'I had it built last year. Had the old yard razed to the ground — good riddance. Of course I had endless battles with the planning people and local residents. But I fought on; only the best for my horses.'

As he waved his arm at the horses' heads, a large black horse backed away, showing the whites of its eyes.

'Who's that?' Sasha didn't like to see a horse so wary of humans.

'Oh, that's Jewel. Crown Jewel is his registered name. He's had a long sad history — five owners in less than two years. Everyone's had to give up on him. In fact he was destined for the knackers before I took him on a month or so ago. And I'm not going to give up, however long it takes.' He had a faraway look in his noble eyes that captivated Sasha.

'I know what you mean,' she said. 'People are so impatient, aren't they? If a horse isn't ready for jumping competitions the day after tomorrow, then the owner gives up and sells it on. But that just isn't right.' She could feel the heat of her conviction racing through her body. 'Horses aren't disposable.'

Guy laid a hand on her arm. 'You know, I think you and I are going to get along just fine. We think the same language. Now — how about I get you Jasmine's tack, and you try her out for me in the school? Would you be up for that?'

'Oh — yes!' breathed Sasha, feeling as if she must have died and gone to heaven.

★ ★ ★

Walking back to Jasmine's loose box from the tack room, Sasha had trouble keeping hold of the heavy bridle; Guy had added an extra pair of reins and a martingale to keep the horse's head down.

'I always think it's better to make use of well-designed tack rather than resort to brute force to control your horse,' he explained. Sasha had nodded, pushing to the back of her mind her belief that patience and good riding would get the best from the highly-strung horse. Still, maybe it was different in the world of showjumping, she thought as she undid the bolts on the door.

Jasmine was standing at the farthest side of her large stable and flicked an ear as Sasha walked in.

'Hello, Jasmine, remember me?' she crooned and the horse moved her neck and stretched her muzzle towards Sasha. 'That's right, it's me. The one who used to look after you.' She lifted her hand to move Jasmine's luxuriant forelock out of her eyes and the horse backed away, nose pointing up to the roof, ears back.

'Jazz — Jasmine, it's okay. What's going on with you?' Sasha stood for a moment, hand outstretched until the horse had settled, uneasy thoughts threatening to cloud her happiness at this opportunity she had been granted. After a few minute's nonsense-talking and gentle stroking, her horse settled down and then, because Sasha was careful to keep her movements slow, she managed to groom and tack up the mare without further incident.

Guy was waiting for her at the entrance to the indoor school. The delighted smile he flashed as she rode towards him alleviated her lingering fears. There was an open quality about him that she took to immediately; the way he wore his heart on his sleeve. Unlike some other men she could mention.

'You look great on her. Much better than I do,' he enthused. 'Get her in and give her a warm-up. I've got a few calls to make.' He stood by the door. 'No signal in here.'

As Sasha walked and trotted in circles and curves, she caught snippets of his conversation, only audible as she crossed the front half of the school. He sounded quite heated.

'Well, if a high-profile win is what it takes then it's got to be done . . . ' and on the next circuit, 'They must be out of their tiny minds replacing an established star with a teenager.' And, once she had broken into a trot, 'It's what I pay you for, isn't it? See to it.'

Although interested in Guy's conversation, Sasha's progress was far from smooth. Jasmine was dancing sideways, backing in short steps, or trying to race out of the school altogether with no regard for her rider. While Guy was on the phone, Sasha snatched odd glances to make sure he was fully occupied, loosened her hold on the horse until she was doing little but balance on her back, and spoke calmly. Slowly Jasmine settled down, but it seemed to Sasha that the horse's training had gone backwards in her new home. It confirmed her belief that the mare had the wrong temperament for a showjumper, because surely a rider of Guy's experience and integrity could only influence a horse for good.

'How are you doing? She looks half asleep. Here.' Guy advanced into the centre of the school with a whip outstretched in his hand. Sasha felt Jasmine stiffen, then she lunged sideways with a force that threw Sasha out of the saddle. Even as she flew through the air in slow motion she could anticipate her shame on landing.

'Sasha, I am so so sorry.' Guy spoke with audible sincerity and came down to her level, crouching beside her as she sat up and brushed off the dust. 'Are you hurt?'

Sasha waited until she had regained her equilibrium and then scrambled to her feet. 'Only my pride. She seems much more keyed up than when I last rode her.'

'She's at the peak of condition — that's why. Fighting fit and absolutely raring to go.'

Sasha started to walk towards Jasmine, who was huddled at the far end of the school. 'Next time I'll be ready for her,' she said.

'That's fine, I've seen that you can ride. Why don't you go and wait in the tack room while I sort this feisty horse out?'

Dazzled by his smile, Sasha obeyed as if in a trance.

★　★　★

'Can I make you a proposition?' asked Guy, with a broad grin.

'Go ahead.' Sasha stood by the saddle tree in the tack room, bubbling with excitement at the direction her life was taking.

'Would you like to come and stay here, and learn from me?'

'Oh, yes.' Sasha clasped her hands. 'Tell me I'm not dreaming, please. I can't believe that Guy Palmer thinks I am worth teaching.'

'It's a two-way street, Sasha. I am sure there is much I can learn from you . . . ' He tailed off. 'What was I saying? Right, yes, in return for the instruction you would work for me as a groom.'

Sasha's clasped hands appeared to be praying as she nodded fervently, rapture burning in her eyes. 'That would be wonderful.'

'I can't give you the proper groom's quarters because I've turned it into a holiday let, but I can let you use one of the spare rooms in my house if that doesn't sound too inhospitable.'

'No, of course not! If you're sure you don't mind, that would be great.'

'And in return for the lodgings, you wouldn't mind doing a few of the mundane household tasks? Mopping, washing up, dusting, that sort of thing?' he hurried on. 'My house is crying out for a woman's touch.'

'I'm sure I can help.' Sasha tried to

push the present state of the cottage at Old Oak Stables out of her mind.

'Right — consider yourself hired.'

Sasha couldn't stop herself jumping up and down with happiness, her hands still clasped together. Perhaps everything did happen for a reason: if Seth hadn't have let her down, then she wouldn't have rung Guy; and look what had happened as a result!

'Oh — and by the way, I'm not a great one for red tape. We won't bother with a contract; we know each other and I much prefer to work on trust.' He gave Sasha a look from half-closed heavy-lashed eyes.

'Oh, so do I,' she said, trying to contain her excitement.

'Contracts, term and conditions — ' he spat out the words as though obscene — 'are for people without souls. When you have a special bond like we do, Sasha, you can dispense with trivial details.'

'Aunty! I thought you were back tomorrow.' Although Sasha was only eating a sandwich, she jumped as if she had been engaged in a secret activity when her aunt opened the door.

'I was. I just got a bit bored of hotel life; I found that after a while I couldn't relax. I wanted to be in my own home again.' Aunt Libby wheeled her battered suitcase into the kitchen. 'So, how have things been here?'

Sasha groped for the right words and couldn't find them. 'Oh — okay, you know, just the same.'

'Seth getting on all right? Pulling his weight, is he? Hope so, because it's a lot of work for you on your own. Has he advertised for some help yet?' Libby hung up her waterproof jacket, pulled up the sleeves of her cardigan, sat down at the kitchen table, and immediately it was just as if she had never been away.

'Not sure. He had his big house-warming do, and that took up a lot of his energies and conversation, so I'm not sure what's happened with the recruiting. I talked to someone who might be interested. You know that old pupil of ours? Hannah? The one who got her own pony in the end?'

'Was it a grey Highland? Jester, was he called — is that the one?' Libby was immediately entranced.

'I thought we were talking about the girl — Hannah — not the pony. But yes, that is the one I was talking about. She's back from college and looking for something local. I don't know how long she'd last but she'd be good for short term help.' Sasha wanted to race away with the conversation as a means of avoiding more challenging topics.

'Yes, she'd be good. I still think he should advertise, though. I never had him down as a cheapskate.' Her aunt frowned.

'Aunty, he may well have advertised. I just said I didn't know, that was all.' Sasha rubbed her forehead. 'He hasn't talked about it or the stables the last few days because he was busy with his party.'

'Did you go to it?' Her aunt looked up from the property pages of the local paper.

'Ummm.' Sasha leaned over her aunt's shoulder. 'That looks nice, that two-bedroom gatehouse. Not much of a garden, but then you said you weren't looking for anything too big and the view over the valley would be tremendous. There's the river at the end of the lane as well. And it says it's got an en-suite too.'

Libby scoffed and then pulled her chair out to stare at her niece. 'Are you feeling all right in the head? Since when did I become the sort of person who even knew what an en-suite is, let alone wanted one? And since when did you show the slightest interest in my house hunting?'

Sasha felt like a guilty teenager. 'Just trying to be friendly, that's all.'

Libby gave her a stern look. 'You never answered — how was the party at Seth's house?'

'What are you getting at?'

'You know what I'm getting at. Something's happened between the two of you, I can just tell by your tone of voice, all how-should-I-know whenever I mention him. What's gone on?'

Libby was up on her feet again with her hands on her hips, pawing the ground like a horse. It would have been comical, except that Sasha's secret had scared the laughter out of her.

Sasha sucked in her bottom lip and clenched her eyes tight shut. *Here goes*, she told herself.

'I know you're going to be extremely upset with me, but I have found that I can't work with Seth — it's a sort of clash of personalities. So today I had a chat with Guy Palmer and even rode Jasmine, and he wants me to start up there as soon as Seth will let me go.'

The words shot out of her mouth, and when she had finished she felt inclined to duck. 'And in case you try to persuade me to change my mind, I'm going up there right now to hand in my notice.'

10

As Sasha walked up the drive to Seth's house, she tried to prepare a speech. She didn't want any more misunderstandings or hesitation on her part. Seth had a way of manoeuvring her from her chosen path, and today she wanted to make sure that she got to Guy Palmer's yard as quickly as she could, and without any diversions.

'Seth, I think you know what I'm going to say,' she would begin, and hopefully he'd guess the rest and she wouldn't have to break the news to him at all. And as for the reason — he wouldn't just let her go without a bit of discussion. She didn't want to go all deep and soul-searching with him; she'd done far too much of that already. No — 'Seth, I'm doing this for both of us.' The phrase couldn't sound more noble if it tried.

And then, if all went to plan, they could get onto the practical details: how soon she could leave; whether she could help find him some new staff. And then she could sort out a leaving date. As she walked up the hill, the words clanged in her ears: *leaving date*. She turned round to look back down at the stables in the late afternoon sunshine, swallows swooping above the yard and the younger, hairier ponies playing down by the stream. She drew a ragged breath and started walking again, head held high to stop her lip trembling.

She wondered if Seth would be there. She hoped so; she didn't want to have to do this walk again and it would be a terrible waste of those words she'd prepared; she'd never remember them tomorrow. She hadn't heard his car come past the stables, and it had an expensive, powerful roar about it. She smiled as she thought of that first meeting when she had interrogated James Bond in the yard, barring his way into the cottage. He had been funny then, not taking her too seriously: what was it he had said? *I come in peace.* She felt warm inside at the memory.

He never took her too seriously — that was why they had had so much fun together — all his teasing. What about the time on the log when she thought he was injured? And then she drew in a sharp breath as she relived that first kiss, feeling her stomach muscles clench at the memory. It shouldn't have happened, especially when she was in charge of the horses, but she couldn't deny that it had been wonderful.

She heard a car approaching from the direction of the house and braced herself for a sight of Seth. A small red sports car appeared. At first there was too much sun on the windscreen to identify the driver, and it was only when the car was up close that Sasha recognised Karen behind the steering wheel. She arranged her features into a tight smile and raised her hand, stepping onto the grass for the car to pass.

The car didn't pass. It drew level

with her and stopped. Karen opened the window and turned off the engine. Sasha gave a reluctant glance in Karen's direction and noticed that she seemed different today: hair scraped back into a tight ponytail, pale freckly skin devoid of make-up and a large pair of sunglasses covering her eyes.

'Hi. Just the person I needed to see,' said Karen and removed the glasses to reveal puffy, bloodshot eyes.

Sasha was tempted to ask if the other woman was okay, but told herself it was none of her business. She kept her face masked with that bright smile and waited for Karen to speak.

Karen leaned out of the window, face as close to Sasha as she could manage while staying in the driver's seat.

'Don't tell Seth I've spoken to you. He'd kill me if he knew.'

Sasha felt the usual confusion descend upon her. 'Why?'

'Because he'd say that I'd interfered enough.' Karen gave a few quick nods as if agreeing with Seth.

'I'm sorry, I don't understand what you're talking about.'

'No, not many people do.' Karen gave a wide smile. 'But there's not much to understand here, just that I offered to talk to you and explain that all that scene back at the house was my fault, me just joking around, causing trouble; but Seth didn't want me anywhere near you. In fact he got absolutely furious with me when I suggested it.'

'Why was that?' Sasha felt as if she were stuck at a crossroads.

'Because after being with me for years and not really getting too worked up anything, he's finally discovered someone he is serious about, and I've come along and ruined it for him. And now he doesn't want me causing any more damage, that's why.' Karen's slender body was hanging out of the window as if trying to reach Sasha. Sasha stood on the grass verge gawping at Karen and trying to make sense of her words.

'Serious? Seth?'

'Yes. Seth is serious about you.' Karen said slowly. 'Duh! Isn't it obvious? He's usually unflappable — in all the time I've known him he was, I used to mess around trying to make him jealous and angry and worked up and I never could. He'd just laugh at me. Now look at him. He was pacing around all night after you left. I'd say he's even off his food — didn't touch the takeaway. Although it wasn't especially good.'

'And you and him? Are you moving down here?' Sasha took a step towards the car.

'After the trouble I've caused between you and Seth, I don't think he'll have me near the place again. There's nothing between us, and to be fair, it was always a kind of laid-back relationship. If I'm honest, and I'm trying very hard to be, I suppose that's why I stuck my oar in last night. I was a bit put out that you were stirring up all this emotion in him, when I never could.'

She gave her waterfall laugh, but her

face remained serious.

'It's kind of you to tell me.' Sasha's head was whirling with indecision.

'No, it was unkind of me to mess you about like that.' Karen drew back into the car. 'I'd better get going. I don't want Seth to see me.'

She started the engine and as Sasha watched the car drive towards the stables and off into the sun, she wondered what she should do now. Should she tell Seth the truth? That she'd got a job, but was in two minds about leaving? She needn't say anything about him: just that this stables was her home and she wanted to stay here.

And then, if Seth felt anywhere near as much as Karen had suggested, their relationship would fall into place. Maybe this time she could be a little bit more trusting, and perhaps he could take things a bit more slowly, and then possibly in the end they could be happy together. She sighed and, feeling all her usual fears beginning to accumulate, marched on up the hill.

Sasha tried to pull the bell chain gently to achieve a softer summoning for Seth. She didn't want to get his back up before he'd even answered the door. But, however light her touch, the bell still boomed outside and inside the imposing stone house. She tapped her foot on the floor with nerves. Seth usually answered very quickly. Maybe he'd seen who it was and was lying low upstairs.

Eventually she heard footsteps and Seth's voice: she couldn't hear what he was saying but she'd obviously disturbed him.

He opened the door, dressed in jeans and a sparkling white T-shirt which clung to his chest in all the right places. *Not that he has any wrong places*, thought Sasha, and then bit her lip. The phone was tucked under his chin. He gave her no more than a nod, and held the door open for her to come in.

'I know, Simon. Would you believe

161

it, talk of the devil, she's right here.'
He gave a dry laugh and kept looking
downwards as though concentrating on
the phone. He started to walk into the
kitchen with a wave in that direction for
Sasha's benefit but his face was colder
than she had ever seen it. Sasha followed him, a tight feeling in her chest.

'Yes, yes, it would be good. No, any
time. No, you're welcome. Yes.' Seth
paused in between clipped phrases. Sasha
noticed that his telephone manner was
equally frosty, so perhaps he was just in
a bad mood with the world in general.

'You don't want to speak to her
now?' He turned to glare at Sasha and
then his eyes returned to the phone.
'No, I understand. Choose your moment.
Very wise. Anyway, Simon, I'll let you
get on.' Seth took the phone away from
his face, turned to give Sasha a thoughtful look, frowned and took up the phone
again. 'And Simon, good luck. Hope it
all goes well for you.' His tone of voice
suggested a plague of locusts rather than
any kind of good fortune.

'Funny you turning up now. As you probably gathered, that was Simon.' And when he saw Sasha's look of confusion, his expression become more grim. 'You know — tall, lanky man with the weedy legs and the Adam's apple.'

Sasha wanted to laugh at the description, as she recognised her companion in sparkling wine from the night of the party, but as she glanced up she could not detect the slightest suggestion of humanity in his flinty eyes. Sasha looked up to the ceiling, pretending to be deep in thought. 'Was he that man at your party?' she asked casually at last. 'I never could remember his name.'

'The very same one. He was just telling me what a fabulous time you had together.' Seth's voice was a growl. 'He asked me for your number. He wanted to get in touch with you and pick up where you left off. I didn't enquire where that was exactly but from all his snorting excitement I would hazard a guess that it wasn't separate seats in the cab home.'

'Would you?'

'And I'd like to know something, Sasha, even if we are finished business. It's something that's puzzling me. Why, if you can let yourself go with an idiot like Simon, are you so unwilling to trust someone who's really quite nice, like me?'

'Seth — ' Sasha felt utter frustration take over from her fear. 'We've been through this. We've come out the other side and started on the next argument, or the one after that, it's hard to keep count. But if you do want to revisit the night of the party — I don't, particularly — then let me tell you now.' She stood on tiptoe and shouted. '*Nothing happened with Simon!*' She stood back. 'And no, please — don't give him my phone number.'

Seth rubbed his ear and pulled a mock-grimace. 'You certainly have got a mighty large voice for such a fine-boned little creature, Sasha.'

'And let me ask you something that's been puzzling me, even though we're finished business. Why do you find it so hard to believe someone who's really very nice, like me, when you take the words of an idiot like Simon as gospel truth?' Sasha glared at him.

'So you won't be wanting his phone number, then?' said Seth, his eyes marginally less flinty. 'He wants me to give you work, home and mobile and times when he is available at each.'

'No, I won't. And let me tell you something else — ' Sasha stepped forward and Seth flinched, ducked and grabbed hold of his ears.

'Please don't shout again, Sasha. I believe everything you say, honestly. Just please spare my ears.'

Sasha started to laugh. Seth stood up and gave a long-awaited smile that seemed to light up the dark hall.

'Shall we go somewhere a bit friendlier now?' he asked mildly.

'That would be nice, if you've got the time.' Sasha followed him into the homely kitchen and immediately sat down at the table.

'Do you want anything to drink? Tea, coffee . . . sparkling wine?'

'Can you just shut up about the other night now? Please?' Sasha felt herself blushing.

She waited for Seth to sit down but he stood where he was, straight and still, at the side of the doorway, watching her. He might have got over the phone call, but he wasn't exactly sunny, thought Sasha, biting her lip. Once she had bitten her lip for a few moments, she moved onto fiddling with her hair, and then twiddling her fingers. Still Seth said nothing. What were the words she had prepared on the way up?

'I think you know what I'm going to say,' she said — now, in Seth's presence, hardly sure herself. Perhaps Seth could explain.

'I've been racking my brains. Like you, I find it hard to keep up with the many stages of our relationship.' He raised his eyebrows and assumed a sorrowful expression, epic gestures worthy of a matinee idol.

'The last time I saw you, I said I thought I needed to leave here and find a job somewhere else,' Sasha prompted in a small voice.

'Oh that's right, yes. At the time I disagreed with your decision but thinking about it now, perhaps you are onto something.' He frowned.

Why was their timing always so out? She wished that, like a pair of musicians, they could work on their pace and then resume. Overtaken with sadness, she managed a brief nod and then continued to recite her prepared lines. 'I think it would be best for both of us.'

'I couldn't agree more. In the brief weeks of our relationship, we seem to have packed in quite enough drama for a lifetime.' He gave a thin smile. 'Life's too short for this kind of upheaval. Like you, I have come to the conclusion that we should quit while we are barely ahead.'

'Well, then, you'll be pleased to know I've got another job. At Guy Palmer's yard. Obviously, he'd like me to start as soon as possible, but I told him you had no one but me helping out and it might take a while.' Sasha's mind raced away with the possibilities that a few weeks' notice could present. They'd be working together, close and alone, and with no pressure of a future, perhaps — maybe — they could get it right this time.

'That's very kind of you, and, by the way, congratulations. Guy Palmer's gain is my loss,' he said in the hearty tone of an employer losing a junior member of staff.

'So will you start advertising?' Sasha felt limp with disappointment.

'I've already got CVs for some trainee groom positions and assistant grooms. I think a couple of them were reasonably experienced. I'll have a look this evening and then get in touch tomorrow to arrange immediate interviews. That way, with any luck, I can let you off the hook fairly soon.'

The Seth Sasha knew had disappeared. In his place was a benevolent businessman with no particular loyalty to any one employee.

'Thanks, Seth.' Sasha stood up. 'I'm sorry it didn't work out for us — working together, I mean.'

'It happens,' said new, businessman-of-the-world Seth. 'But you can rest assured I'll give you a glowing reference any time you want one.'

'Right, I'd better be off then.' As Sasha's mind cast around for reasons she could stay, the doorbell boomed.

'Don't know who that is. A bit remote here for door-to-door salesmen,' Seth said as he left the kitchen. And then she heard her aunt's voice.

'She's here now? That's good. I can kill two birds with one stone and let her know too. The seaside? It was okay, all right, nothing special — sandy and full of sea, that sort of thing.'

They arrived in the kitchen side by side. As Aunt Libby talked, Seth stooped down to her level, a gentle smile hovering across his face.

'Anyway, enough of that. Now I'm

back I'd like to make a suggestion.'

'Fire away,' said Seth, and Sasha winced in apprehension of her aunt's words.

'Well, I've been talking to Sasha and she is adamant that she wants to get on with this new job. No point reasoning with her because she's gone all headstrong on me, got the bit between her teeth, you know.'

Seth maintained the polite smile. 'I do.'

'You're going to be hard pressed to find another Sasha at such short notice and I know she's champing at the bit to move on.' Sasha rolled her eyes at Seth, but he ignored her. 'So I thought I could take over the reins temporarily. That would mean Sasha could make an immediate start and you could take your time finding the right person. How does that sound?'

'Great,' Seth said immediately. 'If you think you can manage. Obviously I'll give you all the help I can but it's your expertise I'm after — you'll have to tell me what to do.'

'I can just sit down and bark out orders while you do the legwork,' said Aunt Libby. 'If everyone's happy with that, I'm willing to start on Wednesday. That'll give me a day to get onto the estate agents and then I can get stuck in. We don't really need a changeover, do we, Sasha? Nothing you need to tell me that I don't already know, is there?'

Sasha shook her head, struck dumb as she saw an immediate end to any hope of a relationship with Seth.

'That's very kind of you, Libby,' said Seth and turned to Sasha with the same jovial boss manner. 'That means you can get in touch with Mr Palmer and let him know you can start this week. I'm sure he'll be over the moon.'

11

When Sasha arrived at Guy Palmer's stables on her arranged start date, the yard was spotless and deserted. Even the horses seemed uninterested; noses buried deep into their feed troughs, they did not flick an ear at her approach. She called out 'Hello' a few times with increasing volume, but met no response. She decided to try the house.

Her new home was square-built as a doll's house, red brick, modern, and as empty of humankind as the stable. The curtains were open and as she peered into the kitchen she could see a cluttered table, a sink full of washing-up and cupboard doors hanging wide open and empty.

She would have expected Guy Palmer, TV star and showjumper extraordinaire, to have a housekeeper, assistant and fleet of maids. Or, at the very least, a cleaner — he definitely looked as if he could do with one. She remembered with a sensation of vertigo his suggestion that in return for her lodgings, she could introduce a feminine touch to his home. At the time she had imagined scatter cushions and flower arranging, neither of which she was any good at but, looking at the mess, she wondered if his needs were more basic.

She tried another unsatisfactory clack on the letterbox as the doorbell didn't seem to be working, and then gave up and walked back out to the stable. She had got the right day, hadn't she? He couldn't have changed his mind and realised that the yard of Guy Palmer was no place for an amateur, however closely connected with his troublesome horse ... He had seemed delighted when she had rung to say she could start on Wednesday — she could recall the whoop of joy he had uttered before forcing himself to settle down to the practical details of time and location.

She wandered around, alternating between calling, 'Hello, is anyone there?' and trying to pet the horses who either ignored her or pushed their ears back and showed the whites of their eyes. Even her own horse would not come forward. Jasmine moved her ears at the sound of Sasha's voice but would not venture out of the darkest corner of her box, even though a barely-touched feed trough hung on the front wall.

While Sasha was trying to entice Jasmine out of the shadows, she heard laughter coming from the closed tack room. As she neared it she could hear a male voice talking and much female laughter.

'Was His Majesty on a late one last night, then?'

'So we can assume his early morning will start a wee bit later today?'

'Somewhere closer to mid-afternoon, with a stinking hangover and a filthy temper, no doubt.'

And then more laughter.

Sasha gave a sharp rap on the door,

not wanting to disturb their conversation unannounced, and then opened the door. Inside were a middle-aged man and woman, wearing jeans and boots and fleeces, sitting on the wooden floor, mugs in one hand, large sugary doughnuts in the other. At the sight of Sasha, both the red-faced man and the crop-haired woman tossed doughnuts to one side and began to scramble to their feet, spilling much tea in the process.

'Don't get up, please,' said Sasha, when it was too late. 'I didn't mean to disturb your break. I was looking for Guy Palmer.'

The man shrugged his shoulders, 'He's not here the morning — should be in later.' He turned back to a saddle he was pretending to clean.

The woman registered Sasha's lost expression and gave her a friendly smile. 'Can we help at all?'

'I'm supposed to be starting work here today, as a sort of trainee — I don't know my official title, you know how Guy is, he doesn't like all that bureaucracy and — '

'Red tape, yes I do.' As the woman finished Sasha's sentence, the man sniggered.

'The thing is, he told me to come down here this morning and he'd meet me and show me around and get me started. I'm supposed to be working closely with him, you see.'

She could see the woman's mouth twitching and hear the speedy suffocating of another snigger from the man as the woman turned and poked him in the ribs.

'Our Guy is many things, but he's not especially renowned for his time-keeping. Hang on here and he'll be down eventually. Can't say if it'll be this side of lunchtime, but he always gets here in the end.'

'More's the pity,' grunted the man.

'My name's Sue and this one over here, who spouts a lot of rubbish, is James.' Sue gestured to the man with a womanly smile at Sasha.

'And have you worked here long, both of you?' asked Sasha.

'Too long,' said the man.

'Ignore him, I always do.' Sue picked up her doughnut from the floor and resumed eating it. 'Help yourself, there's more in the bag. We always get the mucking out and feeds done and then take advantage of Guy's late mornings.'

'Are there a lot of them?'

'Unfortunately, Guy's not getting the work at the moment and he's not a happy bunny — '

'To put it mildly.' The man turned to give Sasha a wink.

'And when Guy's not happy, he lets everyone know. Even his horses. And when his horses aren't happy, they don't do well at the jumping, and when Guy doesn't win the jumping he doesn't get any TV work, and so it goes on,' explained the woman, licking sugar from her lips. 'You asked how long we'd been here. It's about five years now — we both started on the same day. But how much longer? Well, let's put it this way, we're both looking for something else.'

'I had no idea,' said Sasha, casting her mind back over the last meeting with Guy, looking for clues. 'Why has he taken me on, then? It's hardly a good time.'

This time James' laugh erupted and Sue dug him in the ribs again.

'He likes to have, em . . . younger people around the place,' Sue said.

'Younger women, you mean,' was James' contribution.

'Okay, then, I won't beat about the bush. Sasha, he probably fancies you,' said Sue and picked up a greasy paper bag from behind the saddle tree. 'Doughnut?'

★ ★ ★

'Sasha. I am so sorry I wasn't here when you arrived. I was needed urgently at the television studio for some voice-over. A real bore when that happens.' Guy gave a smile which nearly made

Sasha forget her earlier conversation in the tack room. His eyes shone with a velvety sincerity that made Sasha doubt Sue's words.

'That's okay. I've helped Sue and James with the grooming and got to know the horses a bit. At least I know my way around now.'

They were standing together on the far side of the five-barred gate waiting for Guy to locate his house keys. He dug into the front pockets of his tight-fitting jeans and patted the back pockets, fumbled in his shirt and then flinging both clenched hands downwards in a violent motion, he stamped his foot, face suddenly dark with anger.

'Why is every last thing against me? Even my keys can't do what I want. What the hell is the matter with the world?' He stamped again.

Sasha, alarmed by the outburst, walked a little way towards the house, pretending to watch a sparrow, and then following with her eyes the winding flight of a small butterfly. She heard something chink as she moved her foot and looked down to find a bunch of keys, held together with a medallion engraved with Guy's head.

'Are these what you are looking for?' she called, turning round to see Guy folded over the gate with his arms clinging onto the other side, bashing his head downwards and wailing.

'Guy, I've found your keys.' She moved closer in small steps until she was beside him, tapped at his shoulder, jingled the keys in his ear and then took a large step away for reasons of self-preservation.

He uncovered his face, saw the keys and the transformation to his face was instant: thunderclouds to sunshine.

'Oh thank you, Sasha, and sorry for my outburst. Things are just getting on top of me at the moment. I've got too much work on, too many people making demands.' He stroked her shoulder. 'Anyway, enough of me — let me show you the house. Another victim of my hectic lifestyle, I'm afraid, but I'm sure you can soon get it spick and span.'

Although Sasha thought her own housekeeping skills left a lot to be desired, she looked like a perfectionist compared to Guy Palmer. The hall was filled with paperwork. Letters, statements and even a pile of unopened brown envelopes covered the carpet. Not stacked up or sorted but flung randomly, creased and torn, littering the floor so that only a narrow walkway remained for access.

'I have no vocation for paperwork, as you can see,' was Guy's only comment as they traversed the passageway.

An insider's view of the kitchen was more shocking than her outside glimpse had suggested. It was not just a pile of washing-up, but mounds of crockery covering the worktops, food encrusted on to the surfaces, and mould growing out of discarded tins and bowls of food. Sasha stood in the doorway, unwilling to venture any further.

'Might need a bit of elbow grease, but I know you women, you'll get it done in no time,' chirped Guy as he waved round the room. As he moved towards the door he nudged a pile of boxes with his hip and Sasha heard a domino effect of clinking glass. Taking a quick peep into the highest box as she steadied it, she saw rows of clear glass bottles, lids removed and empty. An overpowering smell in the ether above the first box suggested that the bottles had originally contained spirits.

'The living room's over there — but it's just as you would imagine.' Guy's pointed towards the closed door, and Sasha squeezed her eyes tight shut, trying not to visualise what lay beyond. 'I'll show you up to your room now.' Guy's eyes flickered with uncertainty as though a disturbing thought had crossed his mind. 'You are living in, aren't you?'

Even amidst this squalor, his eagerness for her as a housemate was touching. 'Yes, of course. My case is in the car, I'll go and fetch it in a minute,' she reassured him, and followed him up the dusty staircase trying to ignore the red wine stains on the pale carpet.

'This is the spare room. I'm afraid it's a bit dusty. I haven't had guests for a long time. Same old story, can't fit them in with my filming schedule. Even the horses are missing out on my time.' He flung open the door of an inoffensive room papered in neutral shades.

'This is lovely,' said Sasha; it was, compared to the rest of the house.

'Yes, poor old horses aren't getting enough attention, which is of course where you come in. Did I tell you that Jasmine's entered for her first jumping competition in a couple of days? Only a tin-pot event — the Western Farmers' Show — but it'll give her some confidence. If you could get her out on the lunge this afternoon, when you've finished in the house of course? Perhaps the kitchen would be good place to start.'

An operatic aria resounded from his bulging pocket. 'Will you excuse me? I need to take this.'

He pulled out his phone and answered. 'Hi, so what's the news?' He turned to Sasha. 'My agent,' he mouthed and then sat down on her bed. 'You what? You couldn't? They said what?' he roared as Sasha found her eyes drawn to the middle distance. 'They've chosen Tim Shepherd? What does he know about Arabian horses? Right, yes. Okay. And what about the documentary? You're still waiting. Chase it up, then. You're down this way tomorrow? For sure, call in.'

Sasha could see Guy replacing his phone out of the corner of her eye but was reluctant to turn round. By the heavy sound of his breathing she suspected another outburst was imminent, and so she began to open up drawers and study the storage space of the room.

'I sometimes wonder what I pay these people for,' snapped Guy.

'It must be hard.' Sasha aimed for neutrality.

'It's just that it all seems so arbitrary,' he said, speaking through gritted teeth and then wailed, 'Just so unfair. It's so unfair. There were two projects I was up for, both involving your mare.'

'Jasmine?' Sasha turned and Guy nodded and patted the space on the bed beside him. She perched on the edge, closest to the door.

'Yes — that was the point of her. She was supposed to get me these jobs. Why else would I have bought her?' He looked directly at Sasha as though the question were perfectly reasonable, and then he shuffled closer to her. She moved so that only one thigh was resting on the bed, the other suspended in a sitting position in mid-air.

'What are the jobs?'

'The one I haven't got is a documentary about the hot-blooded horses of the Middle East. It's quite a high-end production, a lot of money pumped into it, more high-brow than my usual jobs. Harvey, my agent, mentioned it a while back and that's when I started looking around for a nice Arabian that I could bring on. I saw Jasmine winning a small show and talked to your aunt. When I heard about her sad past, the ill treatment and everything, I couldn't believe my luck.' He moved a hand toward her thigh and Sasha leaped off the bed.

'Your luck?' she gasped, as she moved onto the stairs.

'That's the other job that's in the pipeline. Actually the one I'm more excited about. I've made a proposal to the same production company who made *Horsing Around*, that they do a documentary on Winter Jasmine, sort of rags-to-riches. How I rescued her from cruelty and turned her into a top jumping horse. Sound good?' He joined her at the top of the stairs and she started to descend.

'But it wasn't you who rescued — '

'Sound good?'

'Wonderful,' she agreed and hurried out of the house.

★   ★   ★

'Homesick already?' Aunt Libby turned down the television as Sasha opened the door.

'No, nothing like that.' Sasha breathed in the smell of the cottage, a mixture of buttered toast, saddle soap and wood smoke from the unswept fireplace. 'You know what it's like when you're packing in a hurry? I forgot the most basic things. I haven't even got any socks to wear tomorrow.'

'How's it going?' Libby gestured to the seat next to her on the sagging chintz sofa. Sasha tried to resist but found herself gravitating to her aunt's company.

'Oh, all right. You know what it's like on the first day learning something. Can't remember half of what's been said and the rest just blends together into a muddle. I'm sure it'll be better tomorrow.' Sasha flopped onto the sofa that was older than her, stroking the pattern of large pink peonies she could remember from her distant childhood.

'You know it's not too late to come back.' Her aunt was staring at the silent television screen.

'Why would I want to do that?' Sasha snapped.

'I'm not saying you do — but just in case, that's all.'

'No, it's fine. I'd be stupid to give up an opportunity to work with Guy Palmer. He's a bit temperamental but the two grooms are good fun and it's great to be able to be close to Jasmine again and look after her.'

'As long as you're happy.'

'I don't think it's a job for me long term, and I'm not sure about the way he treats the horses — he's much more into discipline and showing them who's boss than I thought he'd be — but that's all the more reason to stay and take care of Jasmine, and there's nowhere else for me right now. Anyway, it was you who offered to stand in for me, so that I had to leave here right away.'

'You sound like you're blaming me! Now I'm confused. I thought I was doing you a favour — you said you couldn't work with Seth a day longer.' Aunt Libby turned the television off and faced her niece.

'You were doing me a favour. And no

one is more confused than me.'

Aunt Libby gave her a look from under her eyebrows. 'You know you really could come back. I'm sure Seth would be overjoyed.'

Sasha managed to wriggle free from the sagging sofa, straightened up and turned to her aunt with shining eyes.

'Seth? He wants me to come back? What's he said?'

'What do you mean, what's he said? He hasn't said anything. It just stands to reason that he'd welcome you back. No one knows the horses better than you do, you know the job inside out. He doesn't need to say anything — it's just obvious.'

Sasha slumped back down. 'No, I can't come back. Like I said, we just don't get on. Can't agree on anything, and that's no way to run a business, is it?'

'Perhaps you're right. You know best,' said Aunt Libby and switched the television on again, with the volume turned right up. Sasha noticed how tired she looked — about a decade older today than when she had returned from the seaside, three days earlier.

'How did you find it? Not too exhausting? I hope you had Seth doing all the donkey work.'

'He didn't do a bad job — he's learned a lot since the last time I saw him. You must have been doing something right. And the workmen are getting on well. I can't tell you how happy it makes me to see the old place put right again.' Libby was still looking at the television but there was vigour in her voice now.

'Better than right — it's going to be fantastic.' For a moment Sasha relived the changes she had planned with Seth, and then remembered with a crash that she was no longer a part of them; she had put herself out in the cold.

'You did a good job at the planning stage. Seth's over the moon about it all coming together like this.'

Sasha gave a quick smile. 'Did he say so?'

'Did he say so? He keeps saying it over and over again.' Libby nodded with satisfaction.

'What exactly does he say about it?' Sasha tried valiantly to keep her voice steady.

'Oh I don't know. Just how much he's looking forward to re-opening the stables, having the whole thing up and running, getting going with the riding for the disabled — I think that's the thing he's most excited about, he's been finding out a lot about it.'

'That was my idea,' Sasha squeaked.

'Yes, I know it was.'

'Did Seth tell you that it was?'

Her aunt looked perplexed, 'No, you did. The moment Seth had agreed, you came running to tell me — don't you remember?'

'Umm, yes. It was just that I wondered if Seth remembered,' Sasha said, the corners of her mouth drooping, her shoulders sunk and her slender arms hugged around her chest.

'He hasn't said anything but I'm sure

he does,' Aunt Libby said and then patted Sasha's shoulder. 'He wouldn't forget something as important as that. It will make all the difference to the stables and to the people who can make use of it. There's not another disabled facility for twenty miles.'

'I know. I just wish I could have been there when it was up and running.' Sasha brushed the back of her hand under her eyes and then looked away from her aunt.

'He said he's going to come and see you at your new yard,' said Aunt Libby with a sideways glance.

'Seth's coming to see me?' Sasha's voice rose several octaves.

'Yes, he said he needed to give you something. I told him I didn't know how welcome he'd be dropping in unannounced, and do you know what he said?' Aunt Libby hooted with laughter.

'No, what?' Libby leaned forwards and urged her aunt on, eager for anything he might have said about her.

'That if necessary he'd just have to

buy a jumping horse from the man, if that's what it took to see you.'

'Did he really say that? That he'd buy a horse, just to see me?' Libby grinned from ear to ear.

'That's what he said, love, word for word, that's what he said.' Her aunt turned back to the television her mouth pursed into a smile.

12

'What's going on here? Can all of you people get to work — now!' bellowed Guy as he entered the yard, the following day, well into the afternoon. A heavy wind was blowing and Sasha, James and Sue had spent much of the morning chasing after buckets, guttering and hay nets, all of which were swept away in the gale. As Guy appeared, they were trying to retrieve a ten-pound note, from James' wallet, which had been caught in a gust and was now stuck up against the highest apex of the new stable block, flapping tantalisingly.

James had fetched a ladder and both women were holding it while James climbed. The strong wind was wobbling the ladder despite the extra support and James was taking the opportunity to perform, leaning one way and then the other, and mewing with fear, as the women doubled up laughing.

Guy stomped into the yard with a heavy frown lining his face. Upon hearing the carefree laughter of his employees, his bottom jaw jutted out and the sinews of his neck became ropey strands.

'Can somebody please explain to me what is going on here?' He marched forward and grabbed the ladder from Sasha's hands and then tugged it away from Sue. James lurched, unbalanced, slid down the roof, caught hold of the guttering and pulled it down with him onto the concrete floor of the yard. Out of the corner of her eye, Sasha saw the ten-pound note flutter away into the sky.

'I can't believe you did that,' Sue snapped, hastening towards James.

'Serves him right. It'll teach him not to mess about in working time.' Guy's jaw was still jutting outwards.

James sat up, let go of the guttering and hobbled to his feet. 'That was out of order,' was all he said as he limped slowly out of the yard and climbed into his car.

'Right — you,' Guy pointed at Sue as though she were an object, 'get Moonlight on the walker and then get this yard sorted out. We may have a film crew down here any day now, I'm just waiting on Pete for the go-ahead.' Sue raced after another bucket that was rolling across the yard, and Guy kicked the fallen guttering out of the way.

Yesterday evening Sasha had stayed working at the stables as late as possible, cleaning tack, sorting out grooming kits, anything to avoid coming into the house. When there were no more jobs to do, she had ventured in quietly, tiptoeing across the hall, hoping that the blaring television in the living room would drown out her footsteps.

After frowning at the kitchen for a few moments, she had forced herself to find a bin bag and collect up the rubbish. Holding mouldy tins and greasy plastic trays by their edges, she had managed to make a sizeable difference to the clutter in a short space of time. Looking round the room for more rubbish, she noticed that there was a large collection of beer cans that had not been present earlier in the day. Finding the sober Guy sufficiently alarming, she had tied up the bin bag and crept up the stairs to her room. Unwilling to forage in the kitchen, her dinner had consisted of a packet of dry roasted nuts and an apple that she had taken from the cottage the day before.

Sasha's eyes darted towards Guy's face. She could discern puffy creases under his eyes that were accentuated in profile, and crow's feet tracking outwards from the corners of his eyes. When her alarm had gone off at six this morning, she could still hear the chatter of the television as she had tiptoed off to the bathroom.

'Right, Sasha, you shadow me.' His phone started singing from his pocket. 'Hold on. It's Harvey,' he mouthed to Sasha excitedly. 'Yup. You're at the gate?

Great, I'll be there. Er, no — the house isn't too welcoming at the moment, got the builders in. Stay in the car and we can go out somewhere.'

As Sasha watched him go, she felt as though she had been granted a reprieve. She stood for a while, letting the full force of the wind catch her face, and then made her way to Jasmine's stable.

* * *

'Friend of hers, are you?' Sasha heard Sue's voice approaching and looked up from Jasmine's straw-encrusted hoof with interest.

'She is a friend, yes, but right now I've come on official business.' Seth's voice sounded even more poised and steadfast, ringing out in this God-forsaken place. Sasha put down Jasmine's hoof, and moved to the stable door, leaning over the bottom half.

'She's around somewhere — unless she's been blown away in the breeze,' said Sue with a chuckle.

'You call this a breeze? Where I'm from, we'd classify this as a hurricane. Might even give it a name.' Seth's voice was getting closer.

'We've got our own human hurricane round here, so natural ones don't impress us much.'

'I won't ask any questions in case you incriminate yourself,' said Seth good-humouredly. 'Have you got anything entered in Western Farmers tomorrow?' He sounded as though he had been attending agricultural shows all his life.

'Just one horse going,' said Sue.

With an instant deluge of happiness, Sasha caught sight of Seth. 'We've got a couple of entrants in the leading rein pony classes so I might bump into you again there,' said Seth to Sue, and as he looked towards Sasha, she observed a blissful smile spreading across his face. Her hand was shaking as she fumbled with the latch to let herself out of Jasmine's box. She stood against the outside door waiting for him.

'Seth, what are you doing here?' She couldn't keep the elation out of her voice and wasn't even sure if she wanted to.

'Official business,' said Seth, grinning from ear to ear.

They stood looking at each other for a minute, a forcefield of excitement fizzing between them, and then Seth stepped forward and took Sasha in his arms. 'I've missed you,' he said. She found herself snuggling closer to him, even though they were already touching, as though trying to become a part of him so that she would never have to let him go again.

'Me too,' she murmured, inhaling the irresistible musky scent of his skin. 'Me too.'

He stepped back and took hold of Sasha's shoulders. 'Official business, remember? This isn't a social call.'

Sasha's rapture slipped away. 'What do you want, then?'

'First, is it okay to talk here? That woman who brought me to you hinted that your boss might not be altogether stable. Hurricane Guy? Is that what she was getting at?'

'Mmmmm,' she said and nodded.

'What was it he called me? A little Hitler, was it?' He dropped his head to one side in a quizzical pose.

'You don't let up, do you?' She aimed a mock-punch at his firm stomach. 'What is it Aunty Libby says about me? That my grandad must have been a terrier. Well, I think I can say the same about you, only an even closer relative — perhaps your mother.'

Seth assumed a stony expression, viewing her through heavy brows in a parody of outrage. 'Are you disrespecting my mother? Calling my mother a terrier? I'll have you know she's is fabulously long-legged and graceful and well-made. In fact more like an Afghan hound than any common ratting dog.'

'If you'd just learn to let go every now and then, I wouldn't have to make these offensive accusations.' Sasha was overflowing with good humour. 'Are you really going to the Western Farmers tomorrow?'

'Libby insisted and I deferred, which is the usual form our working relationship takes. She said if I wanted good publicity for the opening, winning a couple of leading rein classes was how to go about it. She's co-opted a handful of tiny little riders for the day — all better than me, I might add — and she's probably drilling them round the finished indoor school at this moment.'

'Libby says that it's all looking good, almost ready for the grand opening,' Sasha said, without trying to hide her sadness.

'It's fantastic. You should come back and visit sometime. See all your great ideas put into practice,' he said, making Sasha wish that he would stop being quite so polite. 'Or, of course, you could always come back for good. I do miss you, you know. Quite a lot.' His manner was breezy.

'You do?' She maintained a deliberate calm.

'Of course.' His tone faltered. 'I'm sure we could sort something out. Define our areas of responsibility so we didn't tread on each other's toes. I could even make out a formal job description so that you knew just where you stood.'

'Right — what's this official business, then?' Sasha could feel the frustration building inside her.

Seth picked up a package from beside his feet. Wrapped in brown paper and tied with string, it was intriguingly bulky with a square base.

'Are you ready for it?' His eye contact was fierce.

'Well, I suppose so. Don't know what you're going on about but I'll give it a go.'

Seth crouched down and unwrapped the parcel, wrestling for a moment with the knotted string. 'You'd think someone would have taught me to tie a bow by now,' he joked. Finally, he pulled off the brown paper, trod on it to stop it blowing away, stood up and Sasha gave a squeal of delight and disbelief. A purple velvet cushion, bound at the edge with gold cord, tasselled at every conceivable edge. And balanced on top of it was Anna's second highest pair of heels, incongruous and yet appearing strangely at home.

'You complete fool,' said Sasha, her tone of voice turning her words into a compliment.

'Whosoever these shoes fit will be my lawful wedded queen,' Seth chanted, face deadpan. 'It has taken many moons to find you, fair maid.'

'Many moons?' Sasha snorted.

'Yes, many moons,' insisted Seth with dignity. 'Many moons ago, a beautiful princess came to my ball, bewitched me, got very drunk and left with a friend of a friend of mine, leaving these glass slippers behind. I have searched far and wide, all the corners of my kingdom, to find this fair maid.'

Sasha was convulsed with laughter, tears running down her cheeks, doubled up and breathless.

Seth continued in epic tones, 'You must understand the consequences — if the shoe fits, then you are my true love.' Then he broke into his normal voice. 'And there's no getting away from it, you're stuck with me. Okay?'

Sasha, a huge grin on her face, studied Seth's handsome face, eyes dancing, wide smile displaying even teeth, tawny skin stretched over his wide cheekbones. 'Yes, I understand and that's perfectly fine with me. But it's hard work taking off my riding boots, they're very tight-fitting.'

Sasha struggled, treading on the heel of one boot with the other and then reversing the process with little success until Seth pushed her down and hauled off her boots, taking her woolly socks with them; and leaving her feet, the palest of pink, and ridged from the seams of her socks, finally exposed on the barn floor. Seth knelt down on the floor and it was as his hand took hold of her foot that Sasha remembered quite how ticklish she was. By the time he had wrapped the straps of Anna's second highest heels round her ankles, she was shrieking with laughter.

'A perfect fit,' Seth announced, moved his face closer, and Sasha's head swam and she lost focus as the flecked granite of his eyes melted and merged and his eyelashes brushed her cheekbones.

The door clanked and Guy stormed into the barn.

Sasha sprang away from Seth and began frantically fumbling with the ridiculous sandals, until Seth, cool as a cucumber, undid the buckles, slipped off the shoes and forced on her boots with the socks still balled up inside, all in the space of a few seconds. Both parties stood up, a metre apart, and pretended to make civilised conversation.

'Sasha, can I have a word?' Guy scowled at Seth as he spoke. 'I'm not happy about you conducting your social life on my premises.'

'Mr Palmer,' said Seth, 'I hold my hands up and take the blame for this.

Sasha had no idea I was coming to see her.' He kissed Sasha on the cheek, his mouth resting on her skin for a little longer than would be expected. 'But I'll be on my way now.'

Guy glowered at Seth and then turned to Sasha. 'You can stop work right now. I don't want you using up all your fabulous energy on my horses.' He put a heavy arm around her ribs, tight as a straitjacket. 'Go and get yourself ready for me, darling, I'm going to take you out tonight and treat you like a queen.'

Sasha wriggled out of Guy's grasp and tried to catch Seth's eye, hoping that her anguished expression would portray a realistic impression of the state of her mind; but Seth left the barn, walking fast with his head down, without a backward glance.

Sasha had not idea. I was evening or the too? He hadn't Sasha on the check, his mouth posing, Could. Sasha for a little longer, then would ... I could. That I'll be till any way now.

13

Sasha used the time that Guy had given her for beauty preparations trying to construct a suitable text message to Seth. She didn't want to pour her heart out because she knew that her attempts at sincerity always backfired, but she wanted to reassure Seth that his Prince Charming shoe fitting had been more than an amusing interlude. She couldn't find the right words. Meanwhile she could hear the shower pump running, smell Guy's intoxicating perfume and hear his footsteps moving between his dressing room and his bedroom. And she was still sitting on the bed, wrapped in a damp towel, hair bedraggled, gazing at her mobile and getting no closer to Seth.

Looking at her watch and finding she had fifteen minutes to get ready, she let her phone fall to the floor and searched through the suitcase of clothes that she had no wish to unpack, knowing that she would find nothing dressy or sexy or close to the kind of outfit Guy would require. She pulled out the only dress she had packed; one of Anna's cast-offs. It was a tight, flouncy pinafore dress and the only reason Sasha felt comfortable in it was because it was made from denim. It made her feel pioneering and prairie-girl free and, because it was low-cut, tonight she wore a tight white T-shirt underneath the dress.

At seven-thirty on the dot, the time Guy jokingly said he would call for her, Sasha stepped outside and waited on the landing, but it was another half an hour, during which Sasha decided to clear up the hall, before Guy appeared. Sasha smelled him before she saw him: the scent of burnt leather mixed with sweet spice, clinging painfully to her nostrils and causing her eyes to water.

'Ready, then?' His clothes were clearly designer-made and expensive, even Sasha could see that; a pair of sheeny bronze-coloured trousers, a khaki short-sleeved shirt and a jacket in a shade of greeny-black that Sasha had only ever seen before in the feathers of a bird. The whole effect was opulent and beautiful, but Sasha's wary mind became more alarmed by the effort Guy was investing in the evening.

He didn't look at her as they left the house, his eyes facing forwards, a faint pout on his lips. He carried his arms stiffly as though he were a shop dummy, walking stiffly against the raging wind.

'We're walking,' he said and strode ahead. As Sasha scurried behind, her hair blowing into her eyes, she reflected that, even by his standards, Guy was in a strange mood tonight.

Sasha ran to catch up, and Guy increased his speed. *Why is he taking me out at all?* Sasha wondered. *I might as well not be here.*

'Where are we going?' she asked tentatively.

'To the only place there is to eat in this dead place,' he snapped back and

Sasha decided not to enquire any further.

After a short walk, Guy stopped outside a stone cottage on the outskirts of the village. Without any explanation, he strode to the door.

'What are we doing?' she asked as she joined him.

'Eating — what do you think?' he answered.

'Hello, Mr Palmer, how are you tonight?' asked a blonde woman with cheeks like apple blossom. She gave Sasha a beaming smile. 'Can I take your jacket?'

Sasha handed her jacket to the woman and followed her into a dining room with one long oak table. Sasha admired the exotic wallpaper of humming birds and flowers, but still found herself no nearer to knowing where she was or what she was doing.

'Do take a seat,' said a small dapper man. 'Can I get you a drink?'

'Yes, um, a sparkling mineral water if you've got it.' Sasha sat down.

'And you, Mr Palmer, can I fetch you

a drink?' The small, dark man hovered beside Guy who was staring moodily out of the window, towards a view of a red brick wall.

'Thought you'd never ask.' He squeezed out a smile. 'A large bourbon, please.'

'Of course, Mr Palmer.' The man hurried away.

'Where are we, Guy? This just looks like someone's dining room,' whispered Sasha.

'It is. That's what we have to do for entertainment round here, construct restaurants out of thin air.' He returned to his wall until the drinks arrived.

After taking a large slug out of his highball glass, Guy's demeanour changed. Sasha witnessed the tension drain from his face and a social manner blossom as if by magic. He continued, 'Yes, as I was saying, Rosemarie and Paul open their house up as a restaurant at weekends, and even sometimes in the week if I've got a special date.' He gave Sasha a knowing look.

'I think I've read about places like

this in a magazine.'

'And now you're experiencing it first hand. Stick with me and I can show you a whole range of things that you've never even dreamed of.' He polished off the glass.

Sasha flashed a quick smile. 'Well, it's my riding I'd really like to work on — that and helping you with Jasmine's training, of course.'

'Well you can just tell that mare, since you seem to think you can talk her language, that she had better perform tomorrow at the Western Farmers, or she's dead meat.' He gave a humourless laugh which did nothing to neutralise his venomous tone. Sasha felt a chill of alarm.

'Don't expect too much of her, will you? She's only just starting out — all this jumping is totally new to her. It might take a while for her to get used to it — and then there's the noise of the show that might distract her. Better not to rush her — it all takes time.' Sasha leaned forward, her eyes willing Guy to exercise some patience.

'As it happens, time is just what I don't have.' He gave an assertive wave in Paul's direction, as though he were one of many customers in a busy restaurant. 'A bottle of a good full-bodied red.'

'I know it must be a little bit harder when you're well-known, but everyone understands that a young horse has to be brought on slowly.'

'Look, I know you're just trying to be helpful but you don't really understand what you're talking about,' said Guy dismissively.

Astonished, Sasha felt that this was one insult too many.

'I know I'm not a famous rider, but I do know about young horses — and, anyway, what I'm saying is hardly controversial.'

Guy put up his hands as though to deflect her outrage. 'This isn't a good day for me.'

'But that doesn't mean you have to abandon the most basic principles of horsemanship!' Sasha could feel a couple of days of swallowed retorts rising to the surface.

'The production company have said they aren't interested in the documentary series about Jasmine.' He looked up as the wine was put on the table, took a taste and nodded. 'They say animal cruelty has been done to death, and that people just aren't interested in it any more.'

'But this would have been a hopeful story, watching Jasmine rise to the top after a shaky start!' Sasha began to be outraged on Guy's behalf.

'You try telling the production company that. Perhaps I should employ you as my agent . . . ' His voice became softer.

'But that does mean Jasmine is off the hook? She doesn't need to get good results in record time if no one is watching her.' Sasha felt this needed to be pointed out to Guy.

'If Jasmine doesn't perform tomorrow then she is off the hook permanently.' Guy took a gulp of his wine. 'I have one chance left, with a very small independent company. Harvey spoke to them this morning on the way up here. They are willing to take on the project if the horse can show some real potential. They want her to turn from a nobody into a somebody, not just a badly-treated horse to a happy horse — remember, this is celebrity culture.' He snorted.

'Can I make a suggestion?' Sasha had her elbows on the table and her chin cupped in her hands.

'Go ahead. Be my guest. You are welcome to try, but I probably won't listen to you.'

'Shouldn't you be at home getting an early night and staying off the booze if you want it all to work out well for you tomorrow? It's not just down to Jasmine, is it? In fact, because she's so young, the onus is on *you* to show *her* the ropes. I don't mind calling this a night now.' Sasha tried not to look too eager as she saw a potential end to this date.

The woman with the apple-blossom

skin arrived with two earthenware bowls and a bread basket. 'Your scallops. I hope you enjoy them.' She left discreetly.

Since Sasha had eaten some peanuts and an apple for her dinner the previous night, and a doughnut for lunch, the smell of the creamy sauce made her mouth water and her stomach started to rumble in anticipation. She took a mouthful, forgetting everything other than the food.

Guy pushed his bowl to one side and poured another large glass of wine. 'In answer to your advice, I probably should do as you suggest and abstain from alcohol and binge on sleep, but I have a good feeling about you.' He tried to catch Sasha's eyes but she was keeping her head down, concentrating on the food, amazed that she hadn't realised quite how starving she was.

'Yes . . . I have a feeling that a night with you will bring me all the luck in the world.' Sasha could feel his eyes boring into her as she reached for the bread and simultaneously searched for an answer. 'And I could do with some luck right now.'

Sasha's mind raced in several different directions which showed no signs of joining. She chewed her mouthful, sipped her mineral water and cleared her throat.

'By a night I am assuming you mean more than this dinner?'

'I mean what I say, a night. I think you're a stunningly beautiful woman. I think you have yet to learn the power you have over men, and that makes you, to my mind, even more attractive.' His voice was husky and caressing, but Sasha was finally wise to his tricks; she had witnessed so many of his transformations that she now viewed Guy's charming persona as nothing but a sequence of manipulations.

'Guy, I have to say that a relationship with you was not part of the job I took on,' she started, pushing her chair from the table and staring down at her hands.

'I was careful not to give you a job description precisely because I thought you would perform and excel in so many areas.' His dark eyes were working hard but they had lost their power to bewitch her. 'And who says anything about a relationship?'

'Guy, I came here to look after Jasmine and improve my riding — and hopefully earn some money as well?' She phrased the last part of the sentence as a question. 'So far, I haven't done much of either. I'm not the type of person to leap into bed with a man at the end of an evening's entertainment, however well we got on.'

'Sasha, Sasha, Sasha, perhaps we can just be intimate — look out for each other. We are two single people; what's the sin in keeping each other company?'

He pretended to look puzzled but Sasha could see his eyes darting backwards and forwards as though searching for a better line.

'I hope you enjoyed your scallops?' When the apple-cheeked woman entered the room it was like a breath of fresh air to Sasha.

'Lovely, thank you,' she said, wondering if she could find a way to prolong this woman's presence. But with one arch look from Guy, Rosemarie disappeared as fast as she had arrived.

'Yes, I was asking where was the sin? And another point I would add, perhaps we could just enjoy the closeness, the beautiful intimacy — just hold each other, and no more.' His eyes were still flickering as he spoke in solemn tones.

Sasha burst out laughing, she couldn't help herself. 'Do you expect me to believe that nothing would happen? I know I'm a little bit innocent for my age, but I'm not as gullible as all that.'

Guy looked hurt and turned to his wine. 'You don't think very well of me,' he said after swallowing.

'No, I don't, and if I can be truthful I'll tell you why. It's not just my principles that are stopping me from doing as you wish; the overriding factor is my good taste.' She spat out the words, tired of diplomacy. 'I don't think you are remotely attractive. Yes, at first I fell for your charm and good looks but that wore off pretty quickly, once I witnessed the way you treated people. In fact it's the same way you treat horses — like disposable objects created solely for your pleasure.'

She breathed deeply and sat back but, when Guy said nothing, she continued. 'I am sure that once you were a wonderfully nice man and a superb rider but now you're spoiled. You think everyone should bow down and worship you or snap to attention the moment you demand it.'

Paul arrived with two plates of fish. 'The sea bass,' he said and scurried away as quickly as his wife had done.

Guy pushed the plate away and this time even Sasha had difficulty facing her food. The scallops had satisfied her initial hunger and the atmosphere was not conducive to any kind of pleasure.

Sasha looked down at her plate and thought of Jasmine, forced to perform tomorrow for this tyrannical rider, without the luxury of any kind of argument. She had to find a way to help her tomorrow, and then perhaps she could beg Seth to buy her back — not that she'd be any good in the school, but Sasha could get another job — one that actually paid money this time — and pay Seth back in instalments. She could work on the finer details later. Just now, she needed to placate her employer.

'I'm sorry, Guy. I've said too much, and most of what I've said is untrue and unfair. I'm just confused and tired and need to be on my own right now. And then tomorrow I'll be back to my normal self and able to whisper sweet nothings to Jasmine and persuade her to do her best for you. Can you accept my apology?'

This time it was Guy who refused to meet her eyes. He sighed.

'You don't need to reassure me that your character assassination was nonsense. I can see that you're scared and emotional, attacking under pressure. Forget it; I just thought there was more to you than a frightened little girl, but obviously not.'

'No, I'm very unworldly. I'm sorry to disappoint you,' she said, and began to dissect her fish.

Guy glanced through her and towards the door. 'Excuse me a moment,' he said and left the room.

Sasha gave a huge breath that reached the pit of her stomach, sat back and closed her eyes. She remained in this position for some time, her ears still alert to any sound that might signify Guy's return. At length she heard footsteps on the wooden floor outside, opened her eyes, collected herself and turned towards the door.

It was the woman, smiling, but with a touch of concern evident in her blue eyes.

'Is there anything I can fetch you?'

'No, I don't think so — I mean, what has Mr Palmer ordered? I don't know what he wants to do. Sorry about the fish, it's not that it isn't delicious — I'm just not very hungry now,' she said, almost standing up in her eagerness to communicate with someone other than Guy.

'Mr Palmer? He's left — didn't he say? He said he had a situation he had to attend to urgently — I assumed it was something wrong with one of his horses back at the stable. He paid the bill and rushed off, a little while ago.' The woman's motherly expression was encouraging an emotional response in Sasha. She blinked away her tears and stood up.

'No, he didn't say anything. Never mind. I can make my own way back. At least he didn't leave me with the bill!' She forced a laugh.

'Can we ring you a taxi?'

'No, don't worry. I'll be fine,' she reassured her temporary hostess as she put on her jacket and left.

Once outside Sasha leaned against the wall, finding it hard to keep her balance in the gale. As she clung to the wall, watching a stream of rubbish flow by in mid-air, she tried to decide what she should do. There was no way she was staying another night in Guy's house, and all her impulses were pushing her to phone Anna and ask for a lift home to the cottage. Her own car keys were stuck in Guy's house, along with all her other possessions.

She imagined jumping into Anna's cosy little car, and ranting about her evening on the way home. Her friend would be outraged on her behalf and, as with every other problem they encountered, they would end up joking and howling with laughter.

But leaving the stables now would mean letting down her horse. If she wasn't there tomorrow, looking out for Jasmine, who knew what Guy would do to her? She patted her pocket for her mobile, wondering whether to ring Anna anyway — and then remembered she had dumped it on the bedroom floor.

'Great,' she muttered and began walking, the wind blowing her towards the stables with no effort required.

As she neared the house, she noticed that all the downstairs lights were on. At least that meant that Guy was safely indoors rather than lurking somewhere around the stables. She ducked down as she passed the kitchen window and instead of climbing over the locked five-bar gate, and risking the alarm, she slid through the fence and ran on tiptoe across the stable yard. She had no idea which parts of the stable triggered the alarm system, but since Guy neglected so many crucial areas of his life, she hoped that this was one more task he might have overlooked.

When Sasha saw the barn door not just unlocked, but actually hanging open she felt the tension in her shoulders flop away. She walked into the barn, trying to be quiet now so as not to disturb the horses, grabbed two horse rugs from the feed room, made a bed for herself outside Jasmine's box, and settled down to sleep.

14

Although the barn floor was painfully hard and the rugs full of horse hairs, Sasha slept better than she had done for some time. She jumped straight to her feet when she heard footsteps, brushed herself down and tried to get the horse hairs out of her mouth.

'You're keen! I didn't think you'd be down this early,' remarked Sue.

'I had a bit of a difficult night, to put it mildly,' said Sasha cautiously.

'With Sir Guy, I presume?'

'No comment, but I'm supposed to be going to the Western Farmers and I need to get back into the house to change without meeting Guy. What would you advise?'

Sue put her head on one side and smiled at Sasha. 'I would say grab the key from the box in the feed room and seize your chance now. He is bound to be fast asleep. If you just creep in and grab your things, you can change down here. Even have a wash, if you don't mind the cold water — it'll wake you up, anyway.'

Sasha found herself hugging Sue. 'Thank you so much. You really think he'll be asleep now?'

Sue patted Sasha's shoulder. 'Absolutely sure of it.'

'What time do you think he'll want to leave, then? Surely he needs to get there quite early if he wants to get the horses settled?' Sasha started worrying about Jasmine's performance.

'He'll get there just before the event, he always does these days. I'm taking the horse box, so you can come with me. That way you can avoid His Majesty all morning.'

'You are a complete star, Sue. Have you spoken to James? Is he coming back after yesterday — and the ladder incident?' Sasha looked around at the other horses, wondering who would look after them while Sue was away.

'Yup, he's a glutton for punishment, just like me, and he's coming back.' Sue paused, her face becoming more serious. 'You see, we both love the horses. That's why we stay here. We're always threatening to leave but we never do.'

'I think this is going to be my last day here,' Sasha whispered and glanced over her shoulder.

'It's okay, nobody's listening.' Sue laughed. 'I don't blame you. None of Guy's protegées last long — although they usually manage more than three days. I think you might be a record. I'll ask James later.'

She registered Sasha's questioning face. 'Sorry, it's a bit of a standing joke between us. He's had a whole series of pretty young women through his doors, gazing soulfully into their eyes and promising them the earth. We watch them come and go, sometimes we even have a friendly bet on how long each one will last — ' Sue caught Sasha's indignant expression and hurried on, 'Not in your case, of course — you didn't give us time.'

* * *

Sasha relaxed in the horse box, happy that her preparation for her departure had gone undetected. She had heard Guy's snoring through the thin partition wall as she had packed her possessions back into her case. Shuddering as she walked past the kitchen on her way out, she was relieved that she had found the opportunity to remove all trace of herself from the house. Looking at the old Volvo parked in the drive, Sasha realised that she would have to return for it at a later date. *But I can bring a bodyguard in the form of Anna*, she thought, glowing inside at the thought of her best friend.

The wind had gained in force overnight. Sue had to avoid branches, traffic cones and flying dustbins as she drove the horse box.

'Jasmine's not going to like this wind, it was even unsettling her in the yard here,' remarked Sasha, looking at the rapidly moving trees through the windscreen. 'They might even have to cancel if it doesn't let up. I can't see the jumps staying put.'

'Not to mention the other livestock. I can imagine it carrying off a few small sheep, maybe even a pig.' Sue braked hard. 'What's that? They've closed the road? How am I supposed to get a horse box through that diversion now?'

A fire engine was parked on the far side of the road sign. Sue jumped out of the cab and ran over to the firemen clustered further up the road. After a few minutes' animated conversation she came racing back.

'Apparently a chimney's blown off an old house further up and made a mess of the road. It's going to take them about half an hour to clear it up, they reckon. I'm going to have to backtrack and take the motorway.'

'It's like *The Wizard of Oz*,' joked Sasha, praying that the entire show would blow away. For Jasmine's sake.

★ ★ ★

At the show ground there was much speculation as to whether the main events would take place at all.

'We've had two tents down already this morning,' explained the steward while showing Sue where to park the trailer. 'And lots of the contestants are stuck on the roads due to flying debris.'

'When are you expecting to make a decision, one way or the other?' asked Sasha.

'Closer to midday is what we've settled upon,' said the steward and waved them into a large space.

'Can you take care of Jasmine, while I go and get the entries sorted out?' Sue asked Sasha.

'Of course. I'm going to have to get her out, but she's not going to like all this creaking and whistling of the wind, and the flying objects.' Sasha pointed at a flag that was now soaring through the air.

'Perhaps leave Guy to get her warmed up. I've texted him about the roads and he's already on his way

— should be here soon, since he can fit through the lanes in his car.'

* * *

'You haven't even got her moving yet?' Guy shouted as he peered into the horse box.

'I thought she'd get so spooked by the wind that it might be best to leave her in here for as long as possible.' Sasha tried and failed to meet his eyes.

'You *thought*, did you?' He climbed up and pushed his way past Sasha. She sucked in her stomach but there was still a moment when his body was pressed against hers. 'Cosy, this, isn't it? As for dumping you last night,' he gave her a bright smile. 'I decided there wasn't a lot of point carrying on with the evening when you made it clear that you weren't going to come up with the goods.'

Sasha moved across to Jasmine and started to remove her rug.

'That's it — get her tacked up as

soon as you can. I'm going to have my work cut out with her today.'

As Sasha put on Jasmine's saddle and bridle, Guy lounged against the partition of the horse box, commenting on her actions.

'You're fumbling with those buckles today — a bit shaky, aren't you? You did up the wrong girth strap, didn't you? I'd have thought a woman with your experience would have known better . . . I'm not putting you off, am I?' All punctuated by a sneering chuckle.

At last Sasha finished with the tack and backed Jasmine out of the box. Before they were outside, she could see Jasmine reacting to the howling wind, her ears back and the whites of her eyes showing as she stumbled down the ramp. Reluctantly she handed the horse to Guy and looked around, as she had done all morning, for Aunt Libby and Seth. She could see no sign of their trailer and hoped fervently that they were not among the many contestants unable to reach the show due to the weather conditions.

She reached for her mobile, wondering whether to get in touch, but her aunt didn't have a phone and Seth required something more than a brief enquiry into his whereabouts as an excuse. She couldn't pretend that the whole Cinderella and Prince Charming incident had not taken place; nor would she want to. She put her phone back in her pocket and decided to walk around the contestants' area in case Aunt Libby's small trailer was hidden behind one of the larger horse boxes.

'Where do you think you're going?'

She turned to see Guy, his face already clouded with anger, riding towards her on Jasmine. Sasha felt a choking in her chest at the sight of her horse; that beautiful movement, she really was floating with her neck arched and her golden tail held high. How could Guy ride her with so little appreciation? As she watched he turned sharply and cantered towards a practice jump. Jasmine approached steadily with her ears pricked forward when a show programme, swept up by the wind, whizzed past, inches from her face. Jasmine flung her head in the air to avoid the fast-moving object and crashed into the jump.

Guy, his face eaten up in the ferocity of his scowl, yanked the horse round and cantered back to the trailer. 'Hold her,' he barked, jumped down, rushed inside the trailer and came back with the longest whip Sasha had ever seen. He snatched the reins from the resisting Sasha.

'Hey, get up, stand still, you little beggar!' he roared and reached upwards sharply, causing Jasmine to jump sideways. The horse pawed the ground, nostrils flared and eyes rolling at the sight of the whip. 'I'm going to teach you to make a fool out of me.'

Reacting to his harsh voice, Jasmine's ears went back and she showed the whites of her eyes before backing away. 'You little waste of space that you are, I'm going to teach you a lesson if it's the last thing I do!' Guy anchored his boots into the soft ground and tugged.

The frightened horse couldn't back any further and so to escape the from the sound of his voice and the sharp feel of his hands she reared up onto her hind legs. Her forelegs, pawing the air, missed Guy's head by inches. As he dodged the flying hooves, he dropped the reins so that Jasmine was loose.

Approaching any other horse in such a state would have made Sasha wary but she had known this one from a foal, and felt that they had done much of their learning together. She had to keep her safe if she could.

'Jasmine, it's me, come here,' Sasha said firmly and saw the horse's ears flick forwards in interest as she recognised the soft voice. 'Jazzy, it's okay. Come here.' The horse snorted, but her nose began to lower, her neck stopped trembling and her taut posture relaxed. In one step Sasha had reached the reins and had hold of the horse.

Immediately Guy barged past her

and yanked the reins from her hand. 'You, stay out of it. She needs to know that I'm in charge.' He was spluttering with rage. He raised the huge whip behind his shoulder and was about to swing it at Jasmine's shoulder when Sasha ran between horse and man, and knocked into Guy with a force that caused him to stumble backwards and lose his grip on Jasmine and the whip. Jasmine careered round to the far side of the trailer. Sasha picked up the whip, broke it in half against her knee, and went to find the frightened horse.

It was immediately clear to Sasha that Jasmine didn't know what to do with her freedom. She tossed her head, took a few steps and stood, her eyes rolling to keep watch from all angles in case Guy came towards her again. Sasha checked behind her and approached the horse again. She caught hold of the broken reins, stroked her muzzle and buried her face in the horse's sleek neck, breathing in her sweet scent.

Both Sasha and the horse jumped

when Guy reappeared. Jasmine side-stepped, nose poking in the air, and Sasha managed to keep hold of the horse but turned in the direction of the angry shouting.

'You want to turn this into something serious, do you? You picked the wrong man here because I've dealt with far stronger than you and I've left them trembling.' Sasha could not tell who he was addressing, horse or human, but his voice was so resonant with rage that he sounded like the baddie in a pantomime.

Sasha, herself quivering with adrenalin, was determined to rescue her horse. She turned to look at Guy and her eyes became glued to the stick he was now holding in his hand. The stick was just that; a normal piece of wood from a tree, thick and barbed with the knotted ends of broken twigs; in width, some-where close to a small branch. He pushed it behind his head to aid momentum and then swung it at Jasmine.

Without thinking, Sasha leaped for-ward, grabbed the end of the stick and tugged it from Guy's hand. With another swooping movement she turned to brandish the stick at him. Guy's mouth dropped open and his eyebrows met under the strength of his frown.

'What the hell do you think you are doing, girl?' he roared.

'You step back from this horse and keep well away from her until you've calmed down. If you come anywhere near her with this stick,' she waved the weapon at him, 'then I'll report you straight to the Stewards and the RSPCA.'

'Who do you think you are, telling me what to do?' Guy advanced and wrestled with Sasha for control of the rope and the horse. Shocking herself with the action, Sasha raised the large stick upwards in another threatening gesture.

'Get away or I'll use this,' she hissed.

'You are such a busybody, aren't you? Think you are better than anyone else, and that you've got the right to judge. How dare you? You have no idea of the pressure I'm under right now!' Guy roared.

'Can you stop shouting at this woman? Whatever has happened, I'm sure it can be sorted out without the need for abuse.'

Upon hearing Seth's voice Sasha felt herself go weak with relief. She dropped the huge stick at her feet, her legs began shaking and she no longer felt capable of meeting Guy's eye. All the fight had simply gone out of her.

There was a crackling of the loud speaker and then a voice spoke out. 'We are sorry to announce that the afternoon session of the Western Farmers is now cancelled because of the adverse weather conditions. I repeat, all afternoon events, including the livestock parade and the horse show, will now be cancelled.'

'That's the end of that, I'm free to go. I can get my horse home,' said Guy in calmer tones and snatched the reins from Sasha. 'My horse, remember? My property.'

Sasha watched Jasmine being led away with a sinking heart. She had lost

241

Jasmine again — and all because of her big mouth. Why hadn't she handled it better? If she'd offered to buy the horse, Guy might have co-operated and perhaps they could have negotiated a reasonable price, especially now his television series had fallen through. She looked down with tears flooding her eyes.

'Sasha, that looked pretty nasty. He looked pretty nasty. Busy defending your horse, were you?' Seth asked gently.

Sasha turned slowly in the direction of his voice, found him to be within touching distance and fell into his arms.

'I was trying to get him to stop hurting Jasmine. He was going to use that great big branch on her and I just told him to lay off or I'd call the stewards. And now he's taken Jasmine away . . . ' She was talking into his wonderfully comforting chest. With her face buried in a warm expanse smelling of freshly ironed cotton and warm citrus fragrance, she felt sheltered from everything, including the gale force wind.

'Come on. Libby's back at the trailer with our two ponies. Do you want to come and find her?' Seth spoke into the top of her head since her face was still unreachable. 'Earth to Sasha, Earth to Sasha. Do you hear me?' he said after a pause. 'Are you ready to come out now?'

Tearing herself away from Seth felt like diving into freezing water after a long period basking in the sun. 'Yeah, I'm here, and there's nothing I'd like more than to see Aunt Libby right now.' *Except to stay here with you*, she whispered inwardly. 'And I guess Guy will hand Jasmine over to Sue and head home — the pressure is off her since the show is cancelled.'

Seth put a comforting hand on her shoulder. 'Right, let's get going. It was lovely to rescue you — although you didn't look much like you needed rescuing — but I'm going to have to rush back to my house to take a call

243

from an off-duty councillor about the chances of getting planning permission for an extension to the yard — that's the kind of exciting life I lead these days. And Libby swears she's fine, but she looks done in to me, and if you could drive the trailer home, it would be a big help.'

He was striding ahead of her through the windswept field at a pace so fast that Sasha found it hard to believe that she had ever really had a hold of this dynamic man.

When Libby and the trailer were visible, Seth stopped and waited for Sasha to catch up, a gentle look on his face. 'Sorry for racing and I'm sorry I can't stay. But do you want to tell me what all that was about?'

'We had a bit of a disagreement last night and I chose to sleep in the stables. I think that made his temper worse today.' Sasha gave a watery smile. 'I was planning to leave anyway. I just wish I'd kept control of myself and managed to take Jasmine with me. Since he didn't actually hit her, it would be my word against his if I reported him now — '

Seth's face froze. 'I hope he didn't treat *you* badly.'

'No, no — nothing I couldn't cope with.'

Despite her heartache over Jasmine, Sasha had to stop herself grinning from ear to ear as he strode away; overcome with happiness that he cared.

15

'Ignore this diversion — just keep on here.' Libby waved her arm in no particular direction. 'Then you can turn down that lane that comes out finally by the Horse and Groom, and you'll find yourself back on the Swansby Road.'

'We're taken an hour to do what should have taken about twenty minutes.' Sasha's knuckles were white from gripping the steering wheel and she was leaning close to the windscreen, trying to dodge the flying branches in the road.

'Relax, Sasha. You look like you're riding a horse,' chuckled her aunt. 'You don't need to steer round everything — these are only twigs.'

'When did you get so chilled and cheerful?' snapped Sasha.

'I'm only relaxed in comparison with

you. Can you just calm down? I hate to think what that man did to you to have you in this state.'

'I'm just going to forget all that, and concentrate on avoiding any more fallen bridges and blown-off roofs and getting home in one piece.' Sasha leaned even further forward in an effort to view oncoming obstacles.

'Careful what you're doing, Sash. Your nose'll be touching the windscreen in a minute.'

'Okay, Aunty. It's just that the day seems to have gone on for far too long already and its only the afternoon, and I slept in a stable last night, and I keep wondering what he'll be doing to Jasmine now, and — '

'Sasha, darling?'

'Yes.' Sasha rubbed her temples, elbows still on the steering wheel.

'Can you try to calm down? You'll have smoke coming out of your ears in a minute.'

'Aunt Libby, don't ever retrain as a counsellor, will you?' Sasha managed a weak smile as she rejoined the line of slow-moving traffic heading in the wrong direction for home.

'Thank goodness this road is still open. I could do with getting out of the car sometime tonight.' Libby hugged her chest and winced.

'Should be home soon. Are you okay?' Sasha glanced at her aunt.

'Just a bit of heartburn. Nothing to worry about. It's just that hot dog I had on the way out of the show — about the only stall that hadn't blown away. I shouldn't have gulped it down so quickly.' She laughed. 'You should have had one, was the best I've tasted in years — all organic and free-range, nothing for you to object about.'

'I just didn't feel hungry, that was all.'

'I know — you're all horse-sick and lovelorn.' She patted Sasha's hand.

Sasha started. 'I'm not in love,' she snapped.

'With a horse, you are — that's all I meant.' Her aunt's voice carried a hint of amusement, which was too much for Sasha.

'I know I'm a standing joke for both you and Seth but it would be nice if you could just stop laughing at me, for today at least,' she snarled, and then caught a sight of her aunt's tired eyes and grey complexion.

'I'm sorry, I'm being horrible. I really am incredibly glad to see you, and to drive home with you instead of Guy. It's just that it hasn't exactly been a fun day.'

'Well, I do feel partly responsible. It was me who sold Jasmine in the first place. If only I'd known Prince Charming was going to arrive the next day and save the stables, I would never have done it.'

'Prince Charming? Seth? What do you mean?' asked Sasha, wondering if her aunt knew anything about the shoes.

'Nothing to get heated about. Just my nickname for him — suits him, don't you think?'

'When you get to know Seth he's an awful lot more difficult than Prince Charming, take it from me,' said Sasha grimly, wrestling with the gear stick.

'If the original Prince Charming was passionate — which I assume he was, or he would have bored the pants off Cinderella — then he might have taken some handling.'

'When did you become such an expert on matters of the heart?' Sasha gave a crooked smile.

'I always knew enough to avoid them like the plague. But I do know that they're not supposed to be easy. I watched your mother navigate her way through a series of crossroads with your father, and you remind me so much of her. I wish you could have got a chance to know her — my little sister.' Aunt Libby brushed her eyes with the back of her hand, and cleared her throat.

'I wish I had, too,' answered Sasha quietly. 'But as for affairs of the heart and Prince Charming, I think I'll just stick to horses. They're a lot easier to get on with, and they don't ask difficult questions.'

'Sasha, I know you're joking, but think about what you're doing. You're a lovely girl, and it would be a waste if you ended up on your own like me, just because you weren't brave enough to take an emotional risk.'

'Don't worry about me, Aunty. If Prince Charming finds a shoe that fits me, I promise you I'll give him a chance.' She turned into the lane leading to the stables, enjoying the slow drive round the familiar bends, grateful to be home at last. As she navigated round the last hairpin bend, she jammed on the brakes.

'Oh no! Look at the poor tree.' Sasha gave a wail at the sight of her beloved hollow oak, uprooted and blocking entirely the lane to the stables. 'Think of all the scenes that lovely old tree has witnessed, right back to Queen Victoria and before. That is so sad.'

'And sad for us,' croaked Aunt Libby. 'I was really looking forward to getting out of the car, stretching out on the sofa for a bit, and getting an early night.'

'It's only four o'clock, Aunty. I had thought for a moment that we might actually be able to get home without anything else going wrong.'

'Not today. And unless you feel up to reversing up the lane with a trailer, we're better off getting out here and climbing over.' Libby picked up her jacket and tried to open the car door. 'That's if I can ever manage to get out of here in this wind.' Her aunt pushed with both arms and then jumped back with a small gasp.

'Libby. What's wrong?'

'Nothing to worry about — just that heartburn again. Obviously my body telling me it's too old for fast food, even if it is organic.' She sucked in her breath, clutched her chest and crumpled down in the seat.

Sasha felt herself go cold with fear.

'Aunty . . . I think we should get you to the doctor. I don't have that much medical knowledge, but I do know that chest pain should always be checked out — just in case.'

She jumped out of the car and ran round to the passenger door. Through the window she could see Libby's crumpled position, her face grey and drawn. Worse still, she wasn't arguing about the need for a doctor.

Sasha took out her phone and then dropped it back into her pocket with an exclamation of disgust. 'Phone's got no signal. Why now?'

She walked up to the tree which, even fallen on its side, towered above her head. She sized it up and returned to Aunt Libby.

'I'm going to have to get across the tree, one way or the other, and then ring the doctor for you. I'll be as quick as I can, I promise, Aunty.'

Her aunt nodded faintly. Her eyes were half-closed and her breath came in short, shallow gasps, presumably to cope with the pain. Sasha hated to leave her alone, but could see no other option.

She tried her mobile one more time, found it to be useless and began to climb the lowest part of the tree. She chose the most approachable part, the top of the hollow area where there were crevices and holes in which to wedge her feet. To begin with, it seemed as though she were doing quite well. The first few steps upward were smooth and effortless, and as she approached the top her blood raced with exhilaration. But then, within a finger-hold of the top, without even a creak of warning, the footholes in the rotten trunk crumbled away, and she fell to the lane, jarring her legs but otherwise unharmed.

'Okay, tree,' she said. 'I thought you were my friend. We did spend many happy hours together but I can see that you probably aren't feeling at your most generous today.' She started to laugh, close to hysteria, as she heard herself addressing the fallen tree. 'Right, Sasha, get a grip.'

Was it any better talking to herself? She didn't stop to answer as she dived down onto her stomach and slithered and wriggled under the highest gap between tree and ground. She could smell the damp and then tasted the road. Grit and mud found their way into her nose and mouth. She had to stay on her stomach for a surprisingly long time before she felt the roaring wind above her head once more. Free again, she picked herself up and ran to the cottage.

Some of the horses, heads out of loose boxes, whinnied at her approach but she didn't stop to pat them. She fiddled in her many pockets for the cottage key, panicking as she convinced herself that she couldn't find it. After throwing the entire contents of her pockets out onto the windowsill, she plucked it out from the strange assortment of objects. She could hear her own breathing, shallow and fast, and leaned on the closed door for a second in an effort to collect herself before racing inside and reaching for the phone.

She searched for the local doctor in her aunt's address book, dialled the number but found that for some reason she had been cut off. Instead of repeating the long number, recalling her aunt's face masked in pain, she decided that 999 would not be an overreaction. Putting the phone to her ear, she still couldn't make out a sound. She checked that it was plugged in, tried again; no dialling tone, just silence.

'No, no, no. What is wrong with everything today?'

She tried her mobile one more time but it still had no signal. And then she was out of the door and racing back to the tree, muttering to herself to keep calm at a faster and faster pace.

From this side, it was apparent that the tree had brought down two telegraph poles. Sasha could see disconnected wire flapping in the wind in three or four places.

'That explains that, then,' she muttered grimly and dived underneath the tree once more. This time she got an even larger faceful of mud and gravel, and even had to slide through a huge puddle before she surfaced into the air again.

She could see Aunty Libby through the windscreen of the car; no better, but at least no worse. She walked around the car to the back of the trailer, narrowed her eyes, and peered up the lane with a look of concentration on her mud-splattered face. She studied the lane for the length that was visible; not far, because the sharp bend blocked her view within a few metres. She looked doubtfully at the trailer. If she could manage to reverse round the first few bends, she remembered that there was a pull-in space where she could unhook the trailer.

She grimaced at the backwards view. She had only passed her test on the third attempt and both her earlier failures had been due to errors in reversing; it was still not her strong point. If she backed the trailer into a ditch or got it stuck, she would block her only route back to the main road. If she succeeded, and it was best to be positive, then it was the quickest way to get Aunt Libby safely to the cottage hospital.

She squared her jaw at the dreaded trailer, took one last look at the first sharp bend in the lane, gritted her teeth in determination and marched back towards the car.

'Aunt Libby, more bad news I'm afraid; the phone lines have been brought down by the tree. But don't worry, we'll get you out of here soon, I promise. I'm just going to have to reverse up the lane and back out onto the main road and get you to the hospital. At least that way, you won't have to move and I can be with you all the way.' Sasha had adopted a chirpy voice to break the news, as much for her own benefit as for Libby. She felt that if she mimicked a different person, a competent cheerful person; the kind of person who found it second nature to reverse a trailer up a single track lane in the middle of a hurricane, she might actually take on the persona and acquire the necessary skills.

Aunt Libby groaned, rolled her head upwards, opened her eyes, all in slow movements which suggested searing effort. She clasped her chest and, with much wincing, managed to shake her head.

'Don't be a complete idiot.' Sasha started at the unexpected words. 'You will never in a million years get round the first few bends and if you get the trailer stuck in a ditch then you've blocked the only route out. Don't you dare do that, Sasha.' She spoke in a whisper but was as animated with indignation as she could manage, and had to flop backwards and take several wincing breathes before continuing.

'Go and fetch Seth,' were her last words before she passed out.

16

If it wasn't in bad taste to find relief in the situation, then Sasha was relieved that she didn't need to reverse the trailer up the road; better still, she had been *forbidden* to reverse the trailer. She wiped some dripping mud from her eyelashes, took a deep breath and ducked down once more by the huge trunk. It was the best crossing yet, and as she slid, she considered how strange it was that she had enough experience to rank her slitherings in such a way.

The sloping drive to Seth's house forked off opposite the stable yard. As she turned up the hill she broke into a run, calling for help and holding her mobile upwards. After a few minutes, however, she was too breathless to run and shout, and the black clouds which had blown in to cover the sky now began to tip rain, caught up by the wind in a slant, directly into her face. Her skin stung and the rain on her face melted the dried mud stains which dripped into her eyes and mouth. She put her head down and pushed herself forward, trying to recall the advice her PE teacher had once given the whole class before a sprint on Sports Day, but soon realising that she hadn't listened past the first sentence.

She was down to the fastest jog she could bear, feeling as if all air had been squashed from her lungs. Up the last steep slope and the house was in sight. She just found the energy to push herself up the last slope and collapsed against the door, nose pressed to the wood, gulping to find a breath as she reached out blindly and grabbed the linked chain of the doorbell. The booming was louder than the wind and she felt reverberations run down her body as she lay upright against the door, teetering on her toes.

The door swung open even before the bell had stopped vibrating and she fell through the doorway into warm welcoming arms. She didn't have to open her eyes, she could smell Seth's citrus fragrance and feel the smooth, freshly pressed cotton of his shirt, familiar from the last time she had fallen into his arms a few hours earlier. He embraced her body and head in his chest and she listened to the thud of his heart, drawing grateful breaths of cotton-scented air before she forced herself away from him to stand back.

'Sasha! Whatever's happened to you?' At the sight of her, his eyes registered such deep alarm that she wondered what had become of her appearance.

'It's Aunt Libby. We need to ring an ambulance, quick, Seth. I think there's something wrong with her heart. Please get on with it. I'll explain everything afterwards, but please ring now.' She tried to shout but found that her voice had become husky, from the emotion and exertion, and instead came out as a cross between a squeak and a growl.

'Look, I'm sorry, Sasha, but the

phone's down here and my mobile had no signal last time I looked.' He picked it up and shook his head. 'Where is she? At the cottage? We can drive down and give her a lift to the hospital.'

'No, it's worse than that. That great oak tree has blown over and blocked the end of your drive and the stable gates, so you won't get through in the car. And Libby is stuck in my car on the far side of the tree trunk pointing the wrong way with no way to turn round, and the trailer stuck behind her. She looks so ill and grey and awful, I — '

Seth took her shoulders and turned her around towards the door. 'Stop talking for a minute, will you, and get in my car. I know it won't save much time, but at least we can drive down to the tree.' His tone was somewhere between gruff and gentle.

She stood rooted to the step. Having fixed her mind on this destination it now seemed implausible that she should have to begin the process all over again: down the drive, under the tree, examine the trailer, scrutinise the lane. She gulped and fixed her eyes on Seth; this time she was not alone. Although her feet were unwilling, she forced them forwards until she was back in the blinding rain and howling wind.

She stumbled after Seth to the car. By the time she had opened the passenger door he had already started the engine.

'I'm going to make your car really filthy,' she said ruefully, looking anxiously at his face before she dropped into the leather seat.

'How can you think about dirt at a time like this?' He was checking his rear view mirror, but his voice was amazed.

'I'm not thinking about dirt at all, but I just thought you might be and it would be better if I brought it up in case you were too embarrassed to mention it at a time like this.' As Sasha struggled on with the sentence she watched Seth's eyebrows rise.

'Well, you're very considerate,' he said and swung the car forwards, rain battering on the windscreen as the car raced down the drive.

'It took me hours to get up here!' Sasha exclaimed as, moments later, Seth screeched to a halt by the tree trunk.

'Poor old tree.' Seth jumped out of the car and touched the trunk.

'That's what I said. I used to have tea parties for my dolls inside the hollow when I was little.' She pushed forwards and ducked down until flat on the ground. 'This is the easiest way to get through — I tried climbing but it all crumbled away.' She disappeared under the trunk, face sideways to avoid the puddles and, as she resurfaced, the ground shook under the impact of Seth's weight, leaping from the top of the trunk.

'I'll take the high road and you take the low road,' Sasha heard him mutter as she darted round the side of the car to check on her aunt: she was clearly breathing, but her eyes were closed and her skin was now drained of all colour.

'I take it that the ponies are still in here?' he asked.

'Yes, I didn't think they'd be up to jumping the log,' Sasha answered.

'First thing, I think we should unload them, no messing about with rugs or anything, and let them loose in this field. I know all the fencing's secure because Aunt Libby had me mending it a few days ago.'

'If you open the gate, I'll get them out now.'

Sasha, having reached a point where she was grateful for direction, lowered the ramp, unfastened the ponies, released them in the field, and then slipped round the car to her aunt. 'Aunty — how are you doing? We're going to get you to hospital now. I've got Seth here, so you won't have to put up with my reversing. Old Prince Charming can do it instead.' She gave a burst of laughter which could just has easily have been tears.

'I beg your pardon,' said Seth

quizzically as he unhitched the trailer. 'Prince Charming?'

'Oh, just Aunt Libby's name for you — nothing to do with me. What are you doing? If you take the trailer off it'll just be in our way. That's the whole problem.'

'I thought it might be easier if we pushed it around the first two sharp bends and then I can run back and fetch the car. I don't want to risk getting it stuck in a ditch and cutting the car off completely.'

She nodded. 'Aunt Libby doesn't look any worse, that's one good thing.' She stood at the front of the trailer. 'Shall we get going?'

The first few paces were effortless and then something about the road surface or the camber must have changed because Sasha was grunting and groaning, she could feel her face going red with exertion, but the trailer was grounded. She noticed that Seth seemed able to expend energy without losing his dignity: his biceps bulged, his legs braced, his face taut and grim, beads of sweat forming on his temples, eyes narrowed. When the trailer finally started to move, with a huge jolt it rolled forwards. As the wet metal slipped out of Sasha's grasp, she caught a glimpse of the immense power required by Seth, to keep the vehicle from plunging into the ditch. His eyes were closed and all the force of body and mind seemed to be concentrated into his arms as he pushed the trailer round the bend.

'I'm hoping that's the hardest part,' he said once the trailer was aligned with the lane. 'If we swap sides, you might find it easier.'

And then after more huffing and puffing from her, and more noble displays of fortitude from him, the trailer was round the second bend, the lane stretching straight as far as she could see.

'I can't believe we did that,' she said before discovering that she was talking to no one as Seth had already started back to the car.

'Keys are in there,' she shouted after him. She leaned against the trailer, eyes closed, actually enjoying the sensation of the sheets of rain washing her aching, stinging body. After the frantic exertion of the last hour, it was a luxury to stand still and allow Seth to do the work.

She was startled from her warm trance of gratitude by the whining noise of the engine as the car reversed at high speed towards the trailer.

'Do you mind hitching it back on, Sasha? You've probably had more practice than me,' he shouted out of the window as he braked.

'Of course not.' This was a job that she could do in any state with complete confidence. She pulled the bar through, fixed the chain and was automatically running towards the driver's door when she stopped and diverted herself to the back seat.

'Sorry, do you want to drive?' Seth asked. 'I'm a very well-behaved passenger, no back-seat driving, I promise.'

'Seth, I would not swap places with you if you paid me. You have no idea how incredibly grateful I am that it is you rather than me that is having to reverse this clunky old giant of a car up the lane in an emergency situation in a hurricane, let alone with the added nightmare of the trailer — '

'Has anyone ever told you that developing verbal diarrhoea in a crisis might not be the best mode of survival?' She caught the glimmer of a smile round his eyes in the rear view mirror.

'This is the first real crisis I think I've ever been in, so this personality trait is entirely new to me, I assure you.' She bit her lips shut.

They had moved at least a hundred yards down the lane and Seth was driving fast. In the mirror she watched his expression of casual concentration as he checked both wing mirrors in turn.

'You're good at this,' she observed with admiration.

'I'm sure you can go backwards on a horse.'

'I can — but slowly.' Her mind whirred. 'The horses are late for their evening feed. Poor things must be starving.'

'Don't worry, we'll sort it out,' he said calmly as he pulled into the passing place. 'Can you unhitch this thing again now, and then we can get going properly.'

'Of course. Aunt Libby, can you hear me? Are you okay?' asked Sasha as she jumped out of the car. There was no answer.

Seth touched her hand. 'She's going to be absolutely fine. You've done a brilliant job.'

'Let's not get carried away. You don't know how many more tree trunks might lie between us and the hospital — or the hospital itself might have blown away. I've learned not to get too complacent today.'

* * *

'I'm going to go mad if they keep us waiting any longer.' Sasha jumped off her plastic chair and began to pace the empty waiting room.

'There's never a time when you don't have to wait in hospitals. In fact the longer the wait the better the news, because it means there's no desperate hurry.' Seth waved airily round the windowless room. 'In the meantime, a little more coffee, tea or even soup from the machine? Some cold water?'

'I'm going to scream if you mention these machines one more time.' She paced the circumference of the room.

Seth's dark-fringed eyes followed her progress. 'Sasha, please stop pacing. It's like watching a hamster in a wheel.' He groaned theatrically.

'I just can't stop. I'm useless at sitting still in normal life — that's why it's a good thing I do such an active job — and I just keep thinking about Aunt Libby and how weak she looked when they wheeled her away. If anything happened to her — I can't bear to think . . . ' She leaned against the pale green wall and closed her eyes.

'Wait there. I'll go and ask what's going on.'

A few minutes of waiting while Sasha's imagination ran riot, and then he was back. 'She's stable — that's a good thing, in hospital talk. You can go in and see her now, it's this way.'

★   ★   ★

'Who's doing the horses if you're here fussing around me?' The words were whispered but still spoken with her aunt's recognisable spirit.

'I'll do them when I've made sure you're okay. You've terrified me.' Sasha stared at her aunt, still grey and frail, tucked into a neat hospital bed with wires positioned at intervals across her birdlike chest.

'Oh, Aunty. I'm so glad we managed to get you here.'

'And even though I'm not overjoyed to be here, I need to thank you for that. I know I wasn't exactly the life and soul, but I did take in what a lot you had to go though to get me here.'

'You don't need to thank me, I just wish it had all been a bit easier — you looked like you were having an awful time, while I was busy diving backwards and forwards, under that poor old tree.' Her mouth turned downwards as she remembered the tree.

'You've still got half of it on you.' Her aunt managed a faint smile.

'Haven't had time to look.' Sasha peered in the mirror above the sink and flinched at her reflection. Her skin was covered in a layer of greyish-brown mud, as was the front of her hair which had escaped from its pony tail. She had decaying leaf matter stuck to her forehead and the tip of her nose, and a large scratch across her chin.

'Why didn't Seth tell me? I've been facing doctors and nurses and acting like a normal person. And with Seth as well — this wasn't exactly how I wanted him to see me.'

'Nobody will think any the worse of you, especially not a nice man like Seth.

You know I'm not one to get overly dramatic, but I think it would be fair to say that between you, you saved my life.' Her aunt managed to inject a few seconds of vigour into her speech before she slumped back.

'Do they know what's wrong with you?' Sasha turned her back on the mirror and faced her aunt, a worried look in her dark eyes.

'They think it's angina. A heart condition.' Libby stretched over to give Sasha's scratched hand a comforting squeeze. 'It's not curable but it's manageable. They say they'll have me out of here again in no time, although I might have to steer clear of manual labour for the time being.'

She picked up her water glass but held it still just below her mouth. 'What about the horses? What are you doing wasting time here, when you should be feeding those poor starving horses? It's almost night-time.'

Sasha smiled. 'They are next on the list. Just thought it might be nice to find

275

out how you were, and see if you there was anything I could fetch you before we got onto the horses. It's the kind of thing a loving niece is supposed to do for her only aunty.'

'Now go. You've seen enough of me. I'm in safe hands and you can fetch me my things in the morning. Right now, I'm more worried about the horses. Go on with you.'

Sasha reached down to press a small kiss on her aunt's damp forehead. 'If you're sure — '

'More than sure. Thanks for everything, goodbye.' Her aunt closed her eyes to signify that the conversation was over.

Outside the cubicle, Seth was standing by the nurse's station waiting.

'Everything all right?' He stepped towards her and touched her shoulder. Although his touch was light, Sasha jumped at the feel of his hand on her body which induced recollections of his lips touching her own. She looked down, blushing.

'Sasha, is something wrong?'

'No, nothing. Just Libby being her normal self. Commanding me to stop playing Florence Nightingale and take care of the poor starving horses.' She felt the glow on her cheeks subside as she inspected her slime-covered boots.

'We'll do them together, you can boss me around as much as like, on the condition that after we've finished the horses, you come back to my place, warm up and let me cook you a meal.'

17

Seth turned his key in the door and then made way for Sasha. 'I wish you'd stop looking quite so worried. All I said was that I'd cook you dinner — that's supposed to be a nice thing to do for someone.'

'Oh, Seth, I'm sorry. It's just that I woke up in a stable this morning wrapped in two horse rugs, and since then the day has just got better.' She gave a hollow laugh. 'I've wrestled with a minor celebrity, had to let him walk away with my poor horse again, driven around falling branches, dived under tree trunks too many times to mention. And every time I step inside your house, we find some new way to misunderstand each other. That's actually the bit I'm most scared about.' She bit her bottom lip.

'Look, come into the living room and

sit down — and please don't apologise about the dirt,' he said as Sasha opened her mouth to protest.

Sasha sat down on the darkest armchair, hoping that any leaf matter left on her would blend in with the fabric. She sank back, exhausted, in the upholstery. 'Perhaps I could just stay here all evening with my mouth shut. Then I couldn't possibly offend you.'

'Sasha, I promise not to hurl any unreasonable accusations at you,' said Seth solemnly. 'Is that better?'

'No, because you can still throw any number of reasonable ones.' Sasha spoke with her eyes closed and her head lolled backwards. 'This is so comfortable.'

'I promise not to hurl any accusations at you, reasonable or unreasonable. Anything else?' He was standing beside the armchair looking down at her face.

'Promise not to get all hearty and wish me the best in my new job,' she said, opening her eyes and grinning.

'Have you got a new job?'

'I hope not. Haven't got over the last one yet. Or the one before that — at least you paid me, though.' She looked upwards towards Seth.

'I hope that's not the only advantage I have over Guy Palmer,' he remarked, raising his eyebrows.

'Stop fishing for compliments.' She stretched and yawned. 'I am so exhausted and emotionally drained.'

'You can stay the night.'

Sasha leaped up from the chair. 'No, please don't start all that. I'm going home to the cottage tonight and luckily it's this side of the tree trunk — but if it wasn't, I would still manage to get home somehow.'

Seth's eyes sparkled. 'It was a perfectly innocent suggestion. I have a very nice spare room and I thought that rather than venture out into the hurricane, you might like to stay there. I'm sorry if it's such an alarming prospect for you.'

Sasha touched Seth's hand and met his eyes. 'I'm sorry, Seth. I haven't quite got Guy Palmer out of my system — what an unpleasant thought that he got in there in the first place.' She gave a mock-shudder.

'And just you inviting me back to dinner reminded me of last night, when Guy forced me to go out for a meal with him and then dumped me at the restaurant without a word, because I didn't find his invitation to spend the night with him irresistible.'

She gazed up at Seth, her mouth turning down at the corners. 'I just need to put a night's space between me and that horrible man and then I'll be back to normal again.'

Seth squeezed Sasha's hand, eyes blazing. 'Did he really do that to you? Dump you because you wouldn't — '

'Yes. That's why the stable seemed such a wonderful place to spend the night in comparison.' She smiled feebly.

'I can't tell you how furious it makes me to hear that. If there wasn't a large log between us and the main road, I'd be heading to my car now to go and sort him out.' Although there was laughter in Seth's voice, his jaw was squared and his eyes had narrowed.

Sasha leaned forward and kissed his cheek lightly.

'I can't tell you how good it feels to hear you say that. I feel thoroughly protected and I like it when your voice gets that break in it. It makes you sound very manly and noble.'

* * *

As Sasha padded into the living room, swathed in Seth's huge white robe, she felt strangely vulnerable and shy. She tugged the dressing gown cord a bit tighter and folded her arms across her chest. As her wrist moved towards her face, she sniffed her skin and gave a nervous laugh. Seth, crouched down at the fireplace pouring more coal onto the already roaring fire, looked across questioningly.

'I was just checking to see if I smelled like you. I've tried all your beauty

— sorry, grooming products — I have to say, you have a lot more than me — and I think I've just about rubbed off all the mud and slime and probably the top layer of my own skin with it. In fact,' she looked down at her body engulfed in swathes of white toweling, 'I'm positively shiny with cleanliness now.'

'Come and warm your toes, or perhaps roast them. I got a bit carried away with the fire, and I know spring's not the traditional time for an open fire, but since there are adverse weather conditions, I thought it was probably acceptable.' He grinned. 'Okay, it's any excuse really. I just love fire-building.'

Half an hour apart had given a polite formality to their conversation. Sasha knelt down on the thick rug, as far from Seth as she judged she could sit without drawing attention to the distance.

'This feels a bit odd, doesn't it?' she ventured.

'What? Us? Here?' He looked hurt. 'It feels good to me.'

She knelt down beside him, surrounded by a huge train of bath robe.

'That's just it; it should be wonderful. Me, you; the fire, food; time, space. And yet it feels like we're both missing. The real us, anyway. On our best behaviour, you know?'

'Yes, I know what you mean.' He poked at the fire causing sparks to fly up the large chimney.

'So what shall we talk about? The stable launch? Are you going to have gymkhana games or jumping, or both?' asked Sasha.

'Definitely both. And I'm going to invite the Mayor, I think, as well as all the local press.' He was leaning forward, already warming to the subject. 'And I think we should serve them all cream teas.'

'We?' Sasha found herself saying.

'This is one of those moments where I'm doomed to say the wrong thing, isn't it?' Seth shook his head. 'If I ask you to come back and work, you'll think that I don't care about you as a woman outside the stables. And if I *don't* ask you to come back and work, you'll think I don't care about you at all.'

Sasha looked at him, surprised at his perceptive analysis, and nodded her mute agreement.

'So what am I supposed to do then?' asked Seth.

'Do you want the honest answer?'

'Of course.'

'I have absolutely no idea what you should say, but somehow you need to convey that you can't live or work without me.' The words came shooting out of Sasha's mouth before she could prevent them.

'But I *can't* live or work without you. Don't you know that already?' Seth sounded exasperated.

'No, of course I don't,' said Sasha, but she moved cautiously into a more central position. Closer to Seth.

'What do you think all that shoe stuff was about yesterday? It was me trying to tell you exactly that.'

'Exactly what? Say it,' said Sasha and laughed mischievously.

'I don't want to frighten you off. Every time I explain how much you mean to me, you try to run away and tell me that you are a serious person and that everything needs to happen slowly and that I should calm down so that we can get to know each other and . . . ' His voice trudged through the list of her criticisms.

'Right — okay, back to the stable launch then.' Sasha felt the disappointment as a deep pain in her upper body.

Seth gazed at the fire, watched by Sasha.

'What do you think about cream teas, then?' he said at last.

'Who's doing the cooking? Don't for a minute think that because I'm female I'm going to be baking away for days before the opening. I think — ' She was now crouching closer to Seth, hands gesticulating to demonstrate her strength of feeling.

'Sasha, just give your mouth a rest for

a minute and listen — '

'That's better.' She laughed. 'Your best behaviour is almost used up already. Doesn't last long, does it?'

'No, it doesn't go far, I must admit,' he rejoined, and Sasha noticed that his eyes were crinkled up at the edges in that way she found quite irresistible.

'I think, even if we do have gymkhana games for the younger riders, we should still try to include a fancy dress parade because it will be so much fun for the really tiny ones and it'll generate great pictures for the local papers and maybe TV news.' In small increments she had managed to edge even nearer to Seth, so that her thigh was now brushing against his, creating jolts of electricity through her body.

Seth leaned closer still. 'A fancy dress parade? Is that just as it sounds? Cute children on sweet ponies all dressed up as their favourite fairytale characters?'

'That's right. Like the Three Musketeers or Dick Turpin.'

Seth's mouth twitched. 'Hmmm. Or

Rapunzel, or perhaps Cinderella for the girls.'

Sasha put her hand on top of Seth's and experienced the full force of that familiar heady feeling as her pulse raced, her body warmed, and her nerve endings tingled. 'Seth,' she said huskily. 'I'm ready now.'

'Did I miss something?' he murmured as his arm brushed her waist, generating feelings she could barely contain.

'Just now you told me that whenever you tried to tell me how you felt, you frightened me off by being too serious too soon.' She moved her face up to his so that their lips were within a breath of touching. 'I'm ready now — you won't scare me.'

'I'm glad you mentioned Cinderella,' murmured Seth.

'I didn't — you did, and I'm begging you to be serious now.' She dug her nails into the palms of her hand as his arm touched her hip.

'I am, if you can just listen . . . ' His eyes twinkled but he had stopped smiling. 'The other night — you know, the housewarming party I held here — something funny happened. A stunning girl arrived: I know it sounds fanciful but she was clothed entirely in butterflies, had her hair all pulled up to expose the most graceful neck I have ever seen. Her legs were long and slim like a foal's.' He looked deep into Sasha's eyes. 'You must know what I mean; elegant and awkward all at the same time. I couldn't imagine anyone more beautiful, or funny or kind — really, she was just perfect. We got on like we were made for each other, same sense of humour, understood what made the other tick, how to tease each other. Do you know what I mean?'

Sasha's hands were still engaged in attempting to quell her passion, nails digging into her palms. It was not working. She nodded very slowly. 'Yes, I think I do know what you mean.'

'When she fell into my arms, quite literally, from a very high stool, I never wanted to put her down. I promised her all sorts of stuff — commitment, honesty, and love, and then we had to separate as the other guests arrived . . . and something happened.'

Sasha watched her clenched hands disappear under Seth's clasp. His touch was warm and wonderfully inviting.

'What happened, Seth?' she whispered.

'I got carried away showing off to my London friends, cracking jokes that only we could understand, teasing them about the past. And she got caught up listening to gossip and speculation, especially from Karen, the ex-girlfriend with a gift for drama, who swore blind that I was still carrying a torch for her, of volcanic proportions. And in the end she thought he had lied to her and it was time for her to leave.

'So — ' He squeezed her hand and she could hear the amusement in his voice. 'She got in her carriage with a very strange approximation of Prince Charming and drove away, leaving me heartbroken and lovesick and in her thrall.'

'And then what happened, Seth?' Sasha said softly, her voice frozen with concentration.

'After that, I tried to stop thinking about her and searching for her, but I couldn't do it. She was in my mind every second of the day, I couldn't get away from her and I didn't want to. So I set out to find her, with the only clue I had — the shoes she had left at the housewarming — '

Sasha gasped. 'Oh no — Anna's shoes! I left them in Guy's stable — '

'No, you didn't. They're in the boot of my car.' He looked stern. 'Now you asked for this; let me finish.'

Sasha nodded and settled back against him.

'I found her at the stables of a monstrous ogre, being forced to work for nothing and tend to his every monstrous need.' His mouth twitched but he kept going, ignoring Sasha's hoot of laughter. 'And she tried on the shoe and it fitted perfectly. We were about to walk away into the sunset together, when the wicked ogre summoned a terrible hurricane and snatched the girl away.'

'You can't blame him for that.'

'I can and I will,' Seth said firmly. 'I knew I had to rescue her from the monstrous gorgon.'

'I thought he was an ogre.'

'Both.' Seth held up his hand to silence her. 'But the fair maiden was not only fair and generally wonderful, she was also courageous and resourceful. Single-handed she stopped the ogre from beating a beautiful horse and sent him crawling home, begging for mercy.' He met Sasha's wide eyes. 'Okay, that's poetic licence — but it does sound good. And as I held her in my arms, after witnessing her bravery, my heart swelled and I knew that I was never going to let her go again. That the love I felt for her was more powerful than anything I had ever experienced before, more powerful even than the ogre's hurricane, and that I had to find a way to keep her with me forever.'

Sasha's eyes were wide, her face was still and she remained silent.

'You know, happily ever after.' Seth prompted.

Sasha said nothing.

'Sasha, If I tell you I love you, you're not going to start wailing about taking our time and getting to know each other? Or turn into a pumpkin, or whatever it is Cinderella does?'

Sasha moved her mouth so that it brushed Seth's lips and then gazed directly into his eyes.

'No, Seth, I'm not going to run away or wail or turn into a pumpkin. I'm just going to tell you that I couldn't love you any more than I already do.'

18

'Is that straight now, Hannah?' shouted Sasha, booted feet firmly planted on a step ladder, as she pinned up the second end of the bunting.

'I think so — perhaps up a bit more. That's it — perfect,' replied Hannah, one of the two new grooms, from the far side of the yard where she was filling up hay nets.

'Now the welcome sign,' muttered Sasha, looking at her watch. 'Alex, have you got a minute to help me? And then I've got to chase up Anna for all those scones.' *And I wonder if Jasmine is okay*, she fretted.

Alex, the other young helper, appeared and together they hoisted up the huge sign over the entrance gate. *Welcome to Oak Tree Stables Grand Opening.*

'How long have we got now?' asked red-haired Alex as they both stood back to survey the sign.

'About two hours. Can I leave you two in charge of the ponies and the tack? It all really does need to be perfect. Then I can get on with the other stuff.' She looked at her watch again and then pushed her hair from her face. 'I don't think I'm cut out for this kind of organisational stuff — I'm really not enjoying it. And where's Seth? He promised to be down here first thing.'

'It's going to be fine. It's all in hand. We've almost finished the horses and then all that's left is to tack up and we're finished,' shouted Hannah, now covered in hay.

'Ahh, here he is,' said Sasha, her whole body smiling, immediately reassured by the sight of the dark figure striding down the drive towards the stables. Now she could relinquish control of all the publicity. She watched with pleasure as the silhouetted outline began to transform into the flesh-and-blood Seth: the hint of a swagger suggested in his walk, the angular outline of his broad torso, the length of his legs, luminous grey eyes fringed with black contrasting with the healthy tan of his skin, those full, firm, sensitive lips.

'What time do you call this?' she greeted him, pointing to her watch. 'I'm having a panic attack here on my own wondering — no, dithering — about what to start on next. If you can get on and make all those phone calls to the press, then I can get on with arranging the indoor school for the events. And then I might not have to breathe into a brown paper bag quite yet!'

He watched her with a broadening smile on his sculpted face. 'I'm sorry, Sasha, I'm going to have to love you and leave you this morning.' He stroked her arm with the lightest touch that still managed to generate heat throughout her body. 'It's completely my own fault. I've overlooked something really important and I've got to go and chase it up. I'll be back as soon as I can, I promise — at least by the opening, but probably well before then.'

By the time Seth had finished, Sasha couldn't have opened her eyes any wider. She stood on tiptoe as if to get nearer to Seth's emotional core and her voice was higher still.

'Seth, you can't do this to me! I haven't got a clue what to say to the reporters, I start stammering — you know me — I'll talk a load of drivel like I always do when I'm scared. This is your line of work.'

Seth held up his hands as if stopping the traffic and laughed. 'You'd do it all brilliantly, Sasha. It's not exactly the national press level. But I promise I won't put you through it. I can fit in the calls myself — and I'll be back to handle everything this afternoon.'

Sasha allowed herself to breathe. 'Okay — but what's so important that it can't wait? I could really do with you here.'

'It's a long story and there's no time to explain right now, but I'll make the calls and I'll be back in time. Trust me.'

He kissed her quickly on the lips, causing Sasha's stomach to somersault, and then strode back up the hill, mobile in his hand.

'*Trust me, trust me*. Is that all he ever says?' muttered Sasha, aware as she complained that Seth had never actually let her down. *So far*, she finished grimly.

'Looks like we'll be on our own this morning, ladies. Apparently Seth has some urgent business elsewhere,' she said darkly to the grooms.

'Oh, he's one of them, is he?' laughed Hannah, who had been working at the yard for less than a week.

'One of what?' said Sasha, pulling her crumpled to-do list out of her pocket once more.

'Absent. Gives orders and then runs away having fun for the rest of the day and expects everything to get done, no matter what.'

'No — quite the opposite.' Sasha felt a passionate need to defend Seth against even a hint of criticism. 'He's been working with me from the start, learning about the horses, managing all the work, ordering — he's been great. That's why I can't understand why he has to choose today of all days to go AWOL.'

*   *   *

'Do you think I could have just one scone and clotted cream, since it's such a special occasion?' Libby, wearing a skirt for the first time Sasha could ever remember, was gazing at the cream tea stand longingly.

'Can I trust you to man the stall without eating everything?' asked Sasha, still clutching her now shredded to-do list. 'What would your consultant say?'

'No saturated fat, gentle exercise, fatty fish, get that cholesterol down and keep it down,' chanted Libby. 'It's like being a kid again, all these doctors telling me what to do.' Her face softened into a smile. 'Still, I do want to live to enjoy my retirement. I even went into the

299

travel agent's the other day to find out about cruises. A few of us from the lunch club were talking about booking off-season.'

'And would one of them be a certain silver-haired gentleman from the Old Rectory?' Sasha asked.

'That would be telling.' Libby winked and Sasha scurried on again, eyes fixed on her watch: time was moving at double speed today, she was sure. 'Right, what's next? Indoor school, indoor school.'

'Sasha, you've got a whole load of wood shavings in the back of your hair and your face is covered in dust — you might want to take a look in the mirror,' shouted her aunt. 'And don't worry, everything else is looking great — where's Seth?'

'I wish I knew.' Sasha wondered whether she could fit in a quick trip to the cottage to tidy up. She got out her mobile, dropped her precious list in a puddle, stooped to pick it up. 'I must know it off by heart anyway by now. Seth, Seth, answer your phone. Please!'

Straight through to the voicemail — off, or no signal. What was he doing? When was the last time he'd told her to trust him? At the house warming, just before he started swanning around with Karen and the rest of the London lot and ignoring her. Was it possible, he was just using her: getting the business up and running and then selling and returning to his old life? If that was the case, he'd want to keep her sweet, wouldn't he?

She felt the panic increasing in her chest and tasted fear in her mouth. Hearing a sound, she turned towards the gate and saw the first guests driving under the banner. There were already some horse boxes parked out at the back with competitors for the gymkhana games.

She checked her watch again; forcing her blurred vision to focus on the numbers. Half an hour until kick-off. She steadied herself with a deep breath. Whatever was going on with Seth, she owed it to the stables to pull herself together and make a success of the day. She gave a smile and a wave to the family parking their car, and scurried into the cottage to make herself presentable.

* * *

'Do I call you Mayor, or Mr Mayor or perhaps just Your Majesty?' Sasha gave her brightest smile and led the friendly robed gentleman over to his allotted seat in the indoor school. 'I'm so glad you could come. We've got the gymkhana games first and then a special fancy dress parade of our youngest riders, we're also really pleased that we've a couple of our new disabled riders joining in with this event — look out for a mounted Sleeping Beauty and Superman.'

She caught a glimpse of the large clock on the facing wall. Ten minutes to go; Seth should be here, ready to open the games with his speech. There was no way she could stand in at such short notice.

'If you'll excuse me for a moment . . .'

She moved out into the sunshine and looked around. The yard was sparkling with cleanliness and maintenance. Children were patting the stabled ponies as their parents chatted to the two new grooms. A few guests were already sitting down to enjoy cream teas and, at the back of the yard, small riders were putting the finishing touches to their ponies' appearances, manes plaited, coats gleaming. She looked down at herself for a final inspection: her jodhpurs were spotless, her boots polished to reflect the stable yard and she had sorted out the dust on her face, even finding the time to apply make-up.

She should be proud; everything was perfect. But where was Seth? She couldn't allow herself to accept that he had let her down.

She heard the sound of a smooth car engine in the lane and saw the top of a trailer over the hedge farther up the lane. She sighed — it was no good, he just wasn't coming; better to face it and try to cobble together some speech to open the event. All she had to do was be gracious — nobody liked long speeches, they'd be dying to get on with the gymkhana. Whoever was pulling up in that trailer was certainly cutting it a bit fine — all the entrants had collected their numbers for the gymkhana, as far as she knew.

She turned towards the gate to see the latecomer and felt a physical rush of happiness even before her mind comprehended the sight before her. Seth, in control, just about on time, unbearably handsome, driving his James Bond car . . . which was pulling a trailer.

His window was open as he drove through the gate. 'Help me here, Sasha,' he called. 'Is everything running on time?'

'All except you, yes. What's going on?' She walked level with the window to meet his eye.

'All will be revealed in a minute. I'm sorry, I really didn't expect this to take so long. Roadworks everywhere.' He didn't look guilty or shifty, she had to admit. He got out of the car and, in front of everyone, gave her a long, firm kiss that caused her to reel back into the trailer.

'Seth! We haven't got time for this now,' she whispered as she caught her breath.

'You're right.' He smiled. 'Looks like you've done a brilliant job without me, anyway. Can you give me a hand?'

'If you tell me what it is we're unloading,' she said.

'That would spoil the fun. Open up,' he said standing back, hands on hips, just watching her as she wrestled with the catch.

'Seth, it isn't! You haven't! Seth, you are amazing . . . '

Sasha walked slowly, wonderingly, up the ramp and towards the head of the horse. Winter Jasmine, coming home.

'Are you okay to unload? I've got a speech to make, I'll get it done quickly. Stay right there: just how you are, surprised and grateful — no, I'd even go as far as to say overwhelmed. I'll be right back.' Grinning and impossibly handsome, he loped off towards the indoor school.

Sasha pressed her head into the mare's warm neck, inhaling the scent of summer grass and warm horse. Overwhelmed was an accurate description of her mood: she was deliriously happy but unable to rationalise her good fortune. Having Jasmine back and out of danger was a dream come true, but having Jasmine returned to her by Seth was the kind of fortune she could not have dreamed up.

She leaned against the young horse, and as she took in her circumstances, counted her blessings in disbelief. The beautiful animal snorted and then turned her face to nuzzle Sasha. It was wonderfully quiet and dark in the trailer after the frantic activity of the morning.

'Come on, Jasmine. Let's get you home.' Sasha said at last as she untied the horse's lead rope and backed her down the ramp.

The yard was empty. She could hear the tone of Seth's voice, but not the individual words, and then much laughter, applause and Libby on the loudspeaker calling the contestants in for the first game of the gymkhana. She stood in the sunshine, horse at her side, filled with a warm, delicious happiness as though she had been sunbathing all day, watching for Seth.

As she saw him stride out of the door, her heart lurched and she led the horse forward, first at a walk and then trotting next to her as she ran.

'Steady — whoa, there. Don't want to be mown down.' He was laughing, every part of his face dancing with amusement. She felt the same, sparkling with happiness.

'I'm in complete control,' she said as she hooked a makeshift loop in the lead rein round her wrist, against all health and safety standards, and pressed her whole body against his, arms folded round his chest in a tight embrace. 'I don't know what to say, Seth.'

'How about, 'I am the luckiest woman alive to have a man like you eating out of my hand' or something along those lines?' His voice crackled with humour.

'Well, I am, if you are,' she said, the words muffled in his chest.

'If I am what?'

'Eating out of my hand,' she said, unwrapping herself to study him with a deep gaze.

'I can assure you that there is no one else in the world for whom I would undertake the wild goose chase I have just been on in order to buy this horse.'

'How did you manage it?'

'Short answer is money, lots of it, but I also had to barter and coax and wheedle. If that isn't eating out of your hand I don't know what is.' They were gazing at each other and as if to strengthen the attraction, Seth took her face between his hands, directing it towards his eyes.

'I — I should sort out some way to pay you back. It'll have to be in installments, I'm afraid,' stammered Sasha.

'Sasha, don't you dare do this to me again. What do I have to do to spell it out to you?' said Seth. 'I've got back your horse, not as some sort of business arrangement but as a gift, to show you quite how much you mean to me. I didn't think there was anything I could give you that would mean as much.'

Sasha listened to the words and felt the force of Seth's commitment through the firm touch of his hands on her face.

'Seth, you know me, I'm cautious and cowardly and hard to convince but I think you might have finally got through to me. I love you.' She laughed. 'And I trust you — although I've had my heart in my mouth all morning it's now back in it's right place, galloping away with me. Feel.' She moved closer to him, certain that her heartbeat was already audible.

'And now I've spelled it out . . . will you?' Seth spoke the words to Sasha's upturned face.

'Spell it out a little clearer.' She looked at him playfully, head on one side, smiling.

'Will you marry me, Sasha?' He enunciated clearly, pausing between each word.

'Yes!' she answered and moved her mouth to meet his, lips parting as she gave herself to him.

THE END

We do hope that you have enjoyed reading this large print book.

Did you know that all of our titles are available for purchase?

We publish a wide range of high quality large print books including:
Romances, Mysteries, Classics
General Fiction
Non Fiction and Westerns

Special interest titles available in large print are:
The Little Oxford Dictionary
Music Book, Song Book
Hymn Book, Service Book

Also available from us courtesy of Oxford University Press:
Young Readers' Dictionary
(large print edition)
Young Readers' Thesaurus
(large print edition)

For further information or a free brochure, please contact us at:
Ulverscroft Large Print Books Ltd.,
The Green, Bradgate Road, Anstey,
Leicester, LE7 7FU, England.
Tel: (00 44) 0116 236 4325
Fax: (00 44) 0116 234 0205

Other titles in the
Linford Romance Library:

MELTWATER

Della Galton

When Nina's husband, Carl, dies in a skiing accident she feels that she'll never recover. Carl's twin sister, Ingrid, persuades Nina not to sell the riding stables that she and Carl built up. But whilst the horses help her through the grief — Nina's heart is still frozen. Then along comes Oliver, a motherless child, who communicates far better with horses than people. Nina teaches Oliver to ride but can Oliver and his father, Stewart, teach Nina to live again?

HEARTS IN EXILE

Catriona McCuaig

Two teachers are evacuated from Coventry to the Welsh countryside, where they struggle with wartime hardship as they help their pupils adjust to a different way of life. Will love follow them there? Vivacious Tansy sees marriage as a way to escape her impoverished background, while shy Dinah just wants to find someone to love. She falls for handsome Emlyn, but the young Welshman is equally reserved. How will they ever get together?

A PAIR OF SKY-BLUE EYES

Jasmina Svenne

After two years of nursing the casualties of the Great War, Clara Allingham thinks she is immune to love. But something about the withdrawn Captain William Morton touches her and makes her determined to heal his psychological scars, as well as his physical wounds. However, as the war grinds on, both Clara and William have to choose whether to lock up their hearts and keep themselves safe — or to risk everything for love.